The Secret Life of Lies

Jennifer Gulbrandsen

A Peacock Press Book
Published by Publishing Pen
CHICAGO

Copyright © 2014 by Jennifer L. Gulbrandsen

All rights reserved.

Distributed by Peacock Press, a subsidiary of Publishing Pen, Inc.

Independently distributed by Smashwords, Inc. and Createspace, Inc.

This is a work of fiction. Any similarities to the biographies of persons living or dead is purely coincidental.

No part of this manuscript may be shared, quoted or reproduced via print or other forms of media without the express written consent of the author or Publishing Pen, Inc.

ISBN 10: 1505892708
ISBN 13: 9781505892703

All rights reserved. No part of this book may be reproduced by any mechanical, photographic, or electronic process, or in the form of a phonographic recording; nor may it be stored in a retrieval system, transmitted, or otherwise be copied for public or private use—other than for "fair use" as brief quotations embodied in articles and reviews—without prior written permission of the publisher.

For more information on the author of this book, including media and interview inquiries please visit www.jennibrand.com

This book is dedicated to the messed up 17 year old wreck who first put Ava, Wilcox, Bobby, Justin and Maria on paper alone in her room on an ancient electric typewriter. She knew then she was a writer and the world should have listened. Better late than never, though.
You've come a really long way, kiddo. I'm proud of you.

To Lindi,
Such a treat to sign this for another author!

[signature]

PROLOGUE

Ava awoke to the sound of machines whirring around her. Her vision blurry, she couldn't quite make out where she was. She blinked a few times, and as she did things came into much clearer focus. She was in a hospital bed. She had survived.

She tried to scoot herself up higher in her bed to get a better vantage point of her surroundings, but the second she moved, a hot searing pain ripped through the middle of her body.

"Don't move too much," a voice coming from a shadowy figure sitting in the corner said, "You've been shot."

The figure came out of the shadows and walked over to Ava's bed, pulling the chair he was sitting in behind him. He sat at Ava's side, and she could feel his steel gray eyes piercing into her. Immediately, alarms started to go off as her heart rate climbed to a dangerous speed.

"Settle down," he said leaning back in his chair, "You don't have to worry about what story to tell me, or what lies to keep straight anymore, because the jig is up, Ava. Or would you prefer 'Holly'?"

At that moment a nurse came in, "You're awake! Honey, can you understand me?"

"Yes," Ava answered hoarsely, barely making a sound.

"And do you know where you are?"

"The hospital."

"Do you know your name?"

Ava nervously looked at Agent Wilcox sitting there in the chair. His face betrayed no hint of what she was supposed to tell the nurse.

"Holly. Holly Gordon."

"Great! How are you feeling, honey?"

"Sore, very sore."

"Well that's to be expected. You just relax, and I'll be back with some pain meds in a minute. I should call Dr. Fernhelter and let him know you're up."

"Thank you," Ava said.

The nurse hurried out, and Wilcox leaned against the bedrail.

"I was wondering what you were going to say," he said.

"Fuck you," Ava replied, "Where's Justin."

"He's safe, no thanks to you. Everyone else is dead, no thanks to you as well."

Ava turned her head away, refusing to look at him. Tears welled in her eyes at the thought of what she had done. What she had allowed to happen.

"Listen, Ava. You can be as pissed off at me as much as you want. Had you just listened to me from the beginning, and not gone off the grid, none of this would have happened. I know you've been through a lot, and I know you just wanted to live your life, but I had you set up to keep you safe, and *you* messed that up, not me. I'm sorry about Maria. I will live the rest of my life being sorry that I didn't get to her in time. But if you had even told me there was a Maria in the first place, I would have known there was a Maria to find."

Ava still refused to look at him, Wilcox went on...

"You are the only person who is alive and knows the truth. Justin is alive, but you lied to him so much, he's fucking useless as a witness because he doesn't even know what is real and what is a lie. Like your name, and how you came to be Holly Gordon."

Ava turned her head to look at Wilcox, "So you think I double crossed you? You fucking think I had something to do with this?"

Wilcox paused, "Honestly, no. I don't think that at all. But here's what I do know. I have one of the most ruthless drug lords this country has ever known dead. I have a special agent dead. I have an innocent woman dead. I have a bunch of Bobby's lackeys dead. I have a woman who was supposed to be heading to Connecticut take a left at Chicago along the way and fuck everyone and everything up. I know that because of your dumb ass, instead of sipping Mai Tais on a beach right now, my old ass is back on the job," He sighed and sat back in the chair, looking up at the ceiling, "All I know is I am your best shot right now. It doesn't look good for you at all unless you can make the pieces fit perfectly."

"So what do you want me to do?" Ava asked.

"Tell me everything. The whole thing. I want the whole story, the actual story, the truth, from the moment I rang your doorbell five years ago. Everything. And it goes without saying that if you bullshit me again, you're going *under* the jail. There won't be anything I can do about it."

Ava and Wilcox sat in silence for a while. Long enough for the nurse to come back in with the pain medicine and leave again.

"So what's it going to be, Ava?"

Ava took a deep breath, and used the remote control to raise the head of her bed into a sitting position. An action made possible by the pain meds. She turned her head to face him and looked Wilcox dead in the eye.

"The day you rang my doorbell, the first thing I noticed was your stupid earring..."

CHAPTER 1

I actually thought I was in some kind of Pulp Fiction inspired practical joke when I opened the door to find what looked like Vincent Vega's older brother, and a young Harvey Keitel standing on my porch. Vincent Vega had a graying ponytail, rugged tan, wind worn skin, and a sunglasses tan like he spent the majority of his time riding through the desert on a motorcycle. But my eyes went directly to that stupid earring he wore. A shiny, lame diamond stud in his right ear. Something that was marginally cool back in 1984, but was only cringe worthy on a man old enough to be my father. I must've been staring at him with my mouth open or something, because he flashed his badge about a centimeter from my face.

"Agent Dan Wilcox, FBI. Are you Ava Giancola?"

Immediately my heart began to race, my mouth went dry, and my palms got clammy, "Y-y-y-yes," oh great, I thought. Dad's old mob past has just landed on my front door. Awesome.

My dad was Salvatore Santini. A low level runner for the mob back home in Chicago. Mostly financial stuff, but enough to get him a couple of decades in a federal penitentiary; but all of his stuff happened twenty years ago when I was just a kid. A little kid. The kids don't usually get dragged into this kind of stuff. Mobsters have ethics, after all. No women, no children. My mother died when I was a baby, and my father had a massive heart attack and died seven years into his sentence, so beyond my twin sister Maria getting herself into trouble, which really wasn't that much of a stretch, I had no idea why they would be at my front door in San Diego. I hadn't done anything wrong, but I remembered the day the feds raided our house and took my father away, essentially leaving me and Maria orphaned at the age of seven. So when I see a badge, I freak out.

"Ava," Wilcox began as he snapped the cover over his badge and returned it to his jacket pocket, "I need to talk to you about your husband, Bobby."

"Bobby?"

My husband Bobby was the last name I expected to come out of Wilcox's mouth. Bobby was away on business at a company golf outing in Prescott, Arizona. He was in commercial development, and probably one of the most boring and gentle people on the planet. That's why I loved him so much. After the chaotic life I had lived, he was a safe place.

"Yes, Bobby."

Don't tell them anything. Make them talk to you. If they need to talk to you, they don't have anything. My father's words of warning all those years ago in our kitchen burning papers while Maria and I stood there terrified, rang in my mind. I stood there silent waiting for Agent Wilcox to go on.

"Bobby's out of town again?"

The Secret Life of Lies

"Yes."

"Prescott?"

"Yes."

Harvey Keitel, Jr, who I would later learn was Agent Tim Sorenson, pulled an 8x10 photo out of a folder and handed it to me. It showed Bobby walking through customs at an airport. An airport with Spanish signs.

"What's this?" I asked.

"Yeah...," Agent Wilcox paused, "He's not in Prescott golfing. That right there is your husband, real name Roberto Raul Perez, going through customs in Costa Rica. Where he checks in on the drug cartel he runs between here and there."

I laughed. It was hilarious to me. I don't know, probably a weird response, but WHAT?! Bobby, my Bobby, a good Italian boy who won't even step on a spider is a Costa Rican drug lord? Where are the cameras, because this has to be a prank.

I handed the photo back to Sorenson, "Nice try, guys. You almost had me there. Who sent you guys. Matt? Dave? It was probably Dave, that little shit. Little over the line, even for him."

Sorenson chimed in with a voice deeper and more commanding than I expected, "Ma'am, this is a legitimate investigation, if you'd like we can have a supervisor validate our credentials."

"Well, there has to be a mistake then because there is no way Bobby is involved in any of this. That's insane. Truly. There is no way my husband is even capable of such a thing. He doesn't even speak Spanish."

Wilcox and Sorenson looked at each other and shared a brief, but knowing smile. Almost like they knew I would say something like that. That made me a little nervous. And the fact that they knew he was in Prescott golfing, or supposed to be in Prescott anyway... you can imagine how my guts felt in that moment.

"Ma'am, we have sufficient cause to believe that your husband and Bobby Perez are one and the same."

"Why, is my house bugged? What '*cause*' do you have?"

"I can't comment on an ongoing investigation," He answered.

Which means, *yes*. Fuck.

"Well if you're so sure, why do you want to talk to me?"

"It's standard to interview witnesses."

"Or scare the crap out of me to snitch on my husband?"

Wilcox chuckled, "You watch a lot of TV, don't you."

I rolled my eyes, "Something like that. What do you expect... me to believe all of this? You want me to believe that the man that I've been married to for five years, known for almost ten, live with day in and day out, is leading a double life. Not only a double life, but one where he's a drug kingpin? A man that has never even told me a white lie is deceiving me daily? You have got to be kidding me. We're done here. You've made a mistake, and I'm going to sue your asses the second this gets straightened out. Now get the hell out of here unless you have a warrant. I know my rights."

Wilcox, quiet, looked me in the eye for a second, and reached into his pocket pulling out a business card. He held it out for me and I took it without even glancing at it.

"You do have rights, Mrs. Giancola. If you ever want to continue this discussion, give me a call at any of those numbers. My suggestion is you not call from your cell or anywhere in the house. He's got eyes on you. Especially now that we're here," He put his sunglasses on, "Stay safe, Ava."

I backed into my house and shut the door, the business card already becoming soggy in my wet palm. What just happened? I walked over to the front window and watched Wilcox and Sorenson make their way to the dark sedan parked at the curb. As they pulled away, my phone rang.

My life went completely out of control exactly two hours later.

* * *

Sorenson tossed the file folder onto the dashboard and let out a sigh, "Something's off with that one. She's a little too savvy, you know what I mean? You think she knows Bobby is what he is and she's just gonna play us?"

"No," Wilcox answered, "That was real. We scared the shit out of her. She doesn't believe us. How many times have we been on a doorstep and told Mrs. Jones that Tom isn't a mild mannered accountant? She tells us we're mistaken, Tom coaches fucking little league and helps old ladies cross the street. She tells us to leave, and we give her our card. After that, she looks at her entire life through different eyes and sees what she didn't see before. The car around the corner that only leaves when she leaves, how little mail actually comes to the house, she rifles through the desk and underwear drawers desperate for something that is going to prove us wrong, only what she finds always proves us right, and we get the call. This

Ava is sharp, but she probably took a Criminal Justice class or something. She'll call tomorrow. We got her."

Wilcox adjusted the rear-view mirror and laughed as he spotted a black Escalade on their tail, "And there's Mr. Perez's paranoia now. I bet he's shitting bricks now that he knows we were on his doorstep. Good for the sadistic little fuck."

* * *

When the phone rang immediately after the agents left, I felt my stomach flip and churn with dread. I looked at the display, it was Bobby.

"Hello?"

"Hey honey!" Bobby answered brightly, "Got a little break in the action, so I thought I'd call and check in. How's things?"

"Well...um...any reason why there would be two FBI agents on our doorstep this afternoon?"

Silence on the other end. After a second or two, Bobby cleared his throat and laughed, "What? FBI Agents? What did they want?"

"To tell me you're a Costa Rican drug lord by the name Roberto Raul Perez. They supposedly have a picture of you in customs yesterday. Which is insane because you're in Prescott. Please tell me this is Dave playing one of his pranks. He went a little too far this time."

More silence.

"Bobby? You there?"

"What did you say?" He asked tensely, completely negating that any of this was a joke by a golf buddy of his.

"I told them they were crazy and asked them to leave. So they did."

"I bet that freaked you out," Bobby said, still sounding stressed.

"Sure did," I answered, "Nothing like the feds knocking on your door to get the heart pumping."

"No joke. I'm so sorry, baby. Did they leave a card? I should call right away and get this straightened out."

I looked at the now completely damp and soggy card in my hand, "Yeah. Agent Dan Wilcox. You got a pen?"

"Yeah, go ahead with the number."

"Ok, 619-555-8774."

He read the number back to me, "I'll call right away and get this straightened out. It has to be a mistake. I'm so pissed they scared you like that. They're about to have one hell of a lawsuit on their hands."

"Yeah, no shit. I'm fine though, it just brought up a lot of memories from when my dad got locked up is all."

"Man, I'm so sorry. You want me to come home? If you need me, I'll be on the next flight."

"No," I answered, "I'm fine, you finish your trip and I'll see you tomorrow night, okay?"

"Okay. I love you."

"Love you too, Bobby. Bye."

I was shaking so hard, I could barely tap the 'End' button on the phone. I stood there just blankly staring into space for a while. This wasn't right. Something wasn't right. He called the second the car pulled away. Did that mean the house *was* being watched all the time?

Stop it Ava, you're being paranoid. There's no way your husband is this guy. No way in hell. The FBI makes mistakes all the time. It's just some strange case of mistaken identity.

But they knew he was supposed to be in Prescott golfing.

And Bobby seemed rather non-plussed about the whole thing. He freaks out if he loses a receipt, but the FBI showing up on the doorstep is no big deal?

No. Something isn't right.

I snapped out of my daze and ran up the stairs and into Bobby's home office. I started rifling through drawers and files. I wasn't sure what I was looking for, but I was on a mission. The only thing there was the usual everyday files normal people keep. Tax returns, house paperwork, we paid cash for the house out of Bobby's trust fund.

Cash.

We paid cash for the house.

Like a damn drug dealer would.

Oh. My. God.

I started looking for bank statements from this trust fund. I knew we had a substantial sum wired into our joint bank account every month, but I never saw any paperwork about the trust. Why would I? It was Bobby's. His parents had been killed in a car accident and there was a huge settlement paid out. There wasn't anything unusual about that.

Nothing. No statements. No proof this multi million dollar trust fund even existed.

I had to run to the bathroom and throw up. What Wilcox said was adding up.

I went back into the office. There had to be more, one way or another. I needed something definitive. Anything.

The Secret Life of Lies

At this point, I was pulling the drawers completely out of the desk and looking for stuff that might be taped to the inside of the desk frame. There was a door where you would normally store a hard drive, but we had laptops so we didn't use it. Inside were the typical boxes of checks, business cards, random office supplies, nothing out of the ordinary at all.

For whatever reason, I pushed on the wall at the back of the cabinet. It was a door that popped open to reveal a thick package. Something like an air mail envelope.

I sat back on the floor and put the envelope on my lap. Hands shaking, I opened it. Inside were papers with what looked like offshore bank accounts, and at the end of the pile were a series of photographs.

I stifled a scream at what I saw.

It was a family of what looked to be Latin decent. Executed on the marble floors of a large house. A man in his 30's, what was probably his beautiful wife, and two children, no older than the beginner dancers who still hold their mother's hands on the way to the Tiny Tots class I teach at the studio.

Gunned down in cold blood.

Children.

He killed these babies and their mother.

The women. The children. They're untouchable.

Oh God. I wanted to scream, but I couldn't make a sound. This man I had trusted, shared my life with, the man who knew everything about me, was a monster. I couldn't breathe, the room spun around me, it was just too much to handle. I can't even describe how it felt. Like someone pushing you into an icy lake. The pain is so intense you can't scream.

Then a numbness washed over me. Another thing I can't really put in words. The room went a dull gray, and I put everything back together like I didn't just ransack the place, and made photocopies of the file on our printer, then I put it back in its secret compartment, and returned the false wall to its normal spot. I put the copied contents of the file in a manila folder, and walked zombie-like down the hall to our bedroom. I put the file in my dance bag, zipped it up, threw it over my shoulder and grabbed my purse. I double checked the back pocket of my jeans to make sure Wilcox's card I had tucked in before my little recon mission was still there.

Making my way down the stairs, my knees felt like jello, and my mind didn't feel like it was in control of my body. I opened the garage door, got in the car, and made my way over to the studio.

Checking my mirror as I headed out of our subdivision, I saw something I had never noticed before. A black SUV on my tail.

Of course there was a giant black SUV on my tail. My life was now *Scarface*.

When I got to the parking lot of the studio and turned in, I noticed the SUV swing into the parking lot of the office complex next door and park in a remote spot. It had probably been there every single day for the last four years, and I didn't even notice it. Why would I? I married a guy who built strip malls, not a Costa Rican drug lord.

I locked the car, and made my way into the studio. As always, I was greeted by my assistant Renee, sitting at the front desk manning the phones, and it was oddly comforting to see life as normal going on around me with the sound of ballet music in one room, tiny tap shoes in another, my Russian instructor Svetlana barking out orders to her pointe class... at least this little corner of my world was intact.

Except for the fact that it was now financed with dead children and drug money, and not a trust fund from a man orphaned by a car accident at the age of three. We were orphans. That's what bonded us.

Only I knew now that it was a lie, or not the truth, at least.

Once I made it to my office, I locked the door, reached into my back pocket and took out the card. Picking up the office phone, I said a silent prayer as I dialed the first number listed on it, the one I gave to Bobby. He answered on the second ring.

"Agent Wilcox."

"Hi, this is Ava Giancola. You were at my house earlier?"

"Yes, Ava. Thought I'd be hearing from you. You're ahead of schedule."

CHAPTER 2

Wilcox let out a sigh and smiled wryly, "Salvatore Santini's kid. Christ, Ava. We spent the better part of two years in that safe house together, and you never once told me about having a sister or being Salvatore Santini's kid."

"You're the FBI, wouldn't take a genius to figure that out. Don't you plug names into computers? Ava Giancola spent twenty two years as Ava Santini in Chicago. Not hard to figure out. It also never came up."

"Never came up?" Wilcox asked taken aback, "After all we talked about during that time, you didn't think to tell me about that? I tell you about my life, Rita, Stephanie, all of it, and I heard about your Aunt and your crazy Uncle, and that your parents died when you were little, but never once did you let on that you knew this game as Salvatore Santini's kid."

Ava laid her head back on the pillow. The pain meds were wearing off and a dull ache began to throb on her side, and the tape began to itch a little over her wound. She looked up at the ceiling for a second and drew a slow breath, "It wasn't personal, I don't talk about it with anyone. Bobby was actually the first person I was able to talk about it with, because he was...well I thought he was...in the same boat."

She took her eyes off the ceiling and met Wilcox's, "You don't understand what it was like for all of those years. My whole identity was 'Salvatore Santini's kid.' The knowing nods from everyone, the sympathetic looks from the teachers, it never went away, and that's why I left and started over the first second I could. I just wanted to leave it all behind and be something different. When I principled at the Joffery Ballet, do you know that the entire first page of the review of my first show was entirely about being the daughter of a mobster? I couldn't even dance without carrying Salvatore Santini on my back. So I walked away. I left. No one in California knew or cared. In California, I was just a dancer."

"You could have told me, Ava. I thought you trusted me. I took care of you," Wilcox said softly.

"I trusted no one, Dan. No one. Bobby was the first, Justin was the second, and Bobby ruined it for Justin, I guess."

"You could have trusted Justin."

Ava looked back up at the ceiling, "See, that's where you have it so wrong. This isn't about trust so much as it's about escape. I wanted to escape Ava Santini. I wanted to escape Ava Giancola. I wanted to be normal. Just normal. Quiet and happy. Not the daughter of a mobster, or the wife of a drug kingpin. Just me. I asked for none of this, yet it's somehow my responsibility to carry on? That's some shit."

They sat in silence again. The monitors whirring in the background against the light humming of the florescent lights. A different nurse came in for the shift change, checked Ava, gave her more pain medicine, and when she left, Wilcox again broke the silence.

"I get it, I really do. But what about Maria? It's strange that you weren't close for all those years after you left, and then you put it all on the line to get to her."

Ava didn't say anything, tears began streaming down her face at the mention of Maria's name.

"Not yet," she whispered, "Don't make me talk about Maria yet. Please."

"I won't. Not yet," Wilcox replied, "Let's just keep going where we left off. Are you okay to go on or do you need to rest?"

"No, I'm okay," Ava said as she wiped her eyes, "I guess we're getting coffee at Starbucks now?"

"Yep," he answered.

"That was a bad day," Ava halfheartedly laughed remembering.

"It probably was."

* * *

The Agent Dan Wilcox who met me on my doorstep and the Agent Dan Wilcox who met me at the Starbucks at the corner of the parking lot where my dance studio was, were two totally different people. This Dan Wilcox was more *Hells Angels* in his tattered Levi's and leather vest with a bandana over his long wavy hair; freed from its greased back Vincent Vega ponytail.

"You look different," I said as I sat at the table he had already occupied waiting for me.

"I only wear the monkey suit when I have to make house calls," he said stirring his coffee.

We had a bit of an awkward silence while he finished perfecting his coffee. Three creams and four sugars. I don't know why that fascinated me about him, but it did. Such a sweet coffee for such a rugged guy. It was kind of cute.

"So," he began, "Why the phone call so quickly? I thought I was a mistaken idiot and you were going to sue my ass at the nearest opportunity."

"Well," I said as my heart began to race, "I found this," I took the manila folder out of my bag and handed it to him.

He raised his eyebrows in surprise as he took the envelope. He removed the copies and flipped through them without much emotion. These papers that had completely destroyed me as I sat there puffy eyed and distraught after I had cried my eyes out over the last twenty four hours, he looked at like they were Ikea instructions.

"He just had this laying around the house?" He asked with a suspicious tone in his voice.

"No," I began nervously, "I found it behind a false door in his desk."

"On a mission were you?"

"Maybe."

"Why," he said flatly, "Why if you believe in his innocence so much, did you go on this mission to find something?"

"To prove you wrong."

"Yep," he smiled as he sat back in his chair, took a sip of coffee, and rang a pretend bell in the air, "That's what usually happens."

"Usually happens?" I asked.

"What, you think you're the only one that this has happened to? No. Not at all. You'd be surprised how many women are have been in your position."

Was that supposed to make me feel better somehow? Because it didn't. Not at all.

"Have you talked to Bobby about any of this?" Wilcox asked.

"No," I answered.

"Why?"

Because I've been through this before? My gut already knows when the jig is up?

"We paid cash for our house, cash I thought was from a trust fund that was set up for him after his parents died," I took a sip of my caramel macchiato to clear the bile rising in my throat, "I couldn't find any paperwork for this trust fund in the office. But the routing number that wires money to our checking account every month matches one of the numbers in that file. I also can't find any payroll checks from his job."

Wilcox raised an eyebrow at me, "You sure you're only a dance teacher? That's some pretty good detective work."

"Dead children," I blurted out.

Wilcox looked at me puzzled.

"There are dead children in those pictures. He kills children?"

"If it benefits him, yes," Wilcox answered.

Hot tears stung my eyes upon hearing that. That was my last hope for any kind of doubt in this mess. My husband killed children. The man who cried when his cat died in his arms, executed children. That's a mind blowing concept.

Wilcox had a file of his own he put on the table, "Robert Joseph Giancola died at birth. It's not unusual to have someone illegally assume the identity of a child that dies at birth because a birth certificate is issued and there won't be two people trying to be the same person."

I just looked at him shocked. What?

"Betty and Joey Giancola were killed in a car accident. But Bobby had already been dead for four years when it happened. Bobby take you to the cemetery to visit them often?"

"Yeah," I croaked out, "As a matter of fact, he did."

Wilcox laid a photo on the table, it was the tombstones of Betty and Joey that Bobby and I would visit once a month. I almost couldn't look at them knowing that these people I felt like I knew based on what Bobby would tell me, were absolute strangers who lost their baby and then died together four years later. They didn't leave a child behind, they met one. I felt like I was going to be sick again.

Wilcox pointed to a little cross off to the left of Betty and Joeys final resting place, "That is where Baby Giancola was buried."

My real husband, I thought to myself sickly.

"*Your* Bobby, was born into this. His father was the big guy, and so were his grandfather and great-grandfather. Only by the time Bobby came around, they were able to have legitimate covers for the drug cartel, and send their kids to school in America. Bobby went to school..."

"At Barrington Academy." I answered.

"Yes. They, his father and his family, stole Baby Giancola's identity and made it Bobby's. Bobby then attended the best boarding schools and college here in America."

"So at least that part is true," I said sarcastically. Ok fine, he didn't lie to me about everything. His life from age nine on was probably true.

"How did he live here all of his life, and then become..." I trailed off.

"I don't know," Wilcox answered. "Bobby's father, Juan Ignacio, was no joke, and Bobby probably had to learn how to be ruthless at a young age. It's not unusual for a child to be left alone in a jungle overnight, or starved a little to make them mean. It's kind of like how you take a pitbull puppy and make it a killer. Part of it is genetics, part of it is pain."

"He's a monster, isn't he," I asked.

"Yes, he is. You are not safe. He knows we're closing in and a scared Bobby is a very dangerous Bobby."

"And you're sure this isn't some kind of mistake?" I asked, practically pleading, "Could you have gotten this wrong?"

"No," Wilcox said flatly, but definitively, "No."

"So now what?"

Wilcox drained his coffee cup and set it on the table, "You only have to get through the next twenty four hours. You have to act like nothing is wrong. We'll make sure you're safe, it goes down, and that's it. It's over. I'll take you to a safe house until after the trial, and then you'll go into our protective services relocation program."

"Witness protection."

"Yes."

The Secret Life of Lies

I could feel tears welling up. Everything would be gone. My husband, my house, my studio, my students; it was exactly my childhood all over again. It was happening again. I was an innocent bystander to my whole life imploding for the second time.

"Is it that necessary? Can't I just stay here? He's going to prison for a long time, I can't see why I have to give up my life if he's going to be in prison for a long time."

"You're a big witness, Ava. You are a huge piece to this whole puzzle whether you realize it or not. He will have you killed without even batting an eye. You won't even make it into your driveway once he goes down. You will be dead."

My mouth went completely dry and the tears flowed freely now. This was really happening.

"What should I do?"

"Nothing. We will handle it all from here on out. Who do you want the studio to go to?"

The thought of losing my studio was almost as bad as losing my life. That was the child I hadn't had yet. The one thing I didn't want to leave behind.

"Give it to Renee. She deserves it," I choked out hoarsely.

"Ok," he answered, "When it's over I will take you to a safe house. There will be exactly five minutes to get you out of the house. Be ready." He then went into all of the instructions of what I could and could not bring. What I was to tell people over the next twenty four hours, and all of the other details I hardly heard over the sound of my own beating heart in my ears. Twenty four hours ago I was happy, and now I was no longer a person, but a unit that had to be moved. Life as I knew it was over forever.

Gone in a flash. Here I was in a Starbucks being told that I had to leave it all behind, and I couldn't even say good-bye.

"Hey!" Wilcox half yelled to break my trance.

"Sorry, it's a lot," I stammered.

"I know. But I will get you through it. Trust me. Nothing bad will happen to you, you have my word."

I nodded. For some strange reason, I trusted this man with my life.

* * *

I don't even know how I did it. The hardest part was saying good-bye to Renee at the studio. She had built that business with me and she was the closest thing I had to a sister besides Maria.

"But...but...Ava! Why can't you tell me anything? Are you okay? What is going on!" Renee pleaded.

"You'll know soon enough," I answered grabbing her hands and looking in her eyes trying to tell her with my gaze what I couldn't tell her in words, "I can't tell you. I'm so sorry. You know if I could, I would. I am not trying to scare you or make you worry on purpose. I shouldn't even tell you this much, but I couldn't leave without saying goodbye. Just run things as you would like I went on vacation or something. In about a week someone from the FBI—"

"The FBI?!" Renee yelled.

I squeezed her hands and shushed her, "You have to be quiet. You cannot act like anything is wrong. I am literally trusting you with my life right now," Renee nodded and I took a breath, "Someone will call you and handle all of the business. You will have the studio free and clear. The parents and students will hear what's going on when the media picks it up. This way you can assure them that there is no connection between what happened and this studio. You can change the name, sell and move, anything you want. It's yours," I drew her in for a hug, "I'm not sure if this is goodbye for good, but it's goodbye for now. I won't be able to contact you for a while."

After a minute of tears and an embrace, I left my studio for the last time, and walked to my car. I don't remember the drive home. I was consumed with worry over how I was going to get through the next few days with Bobby. How can I pretend that I don't know what I know? How do I even look at him? I guess I didn't have a choice. I had to find a way.

When I pulled in the driveway, I watched the SUV I had become acutely aware was following me everywhere, turn the corner, and Bobby's car was in the driveway. I had asked Wilcox if Bobby had another family in Costa Rica, and he had said no. I don't know why that was a comfort to me right now, but it was. The weirdest things become important to you when your life is coming undone. Here this man had deceived me the entire time I knew him, murdered children, and built my entire life on a life of crime, and I took solace in the fact that I was his only wife.

The human mind is a bitch, sometimes.

I let myself in the house like it was any other day after a teaching at the studio, and saw Bobby surfing on his laptop at the bar in the kitchen while he ate a sandwich. Upon seeing this, I immediately had doubts about what Wilcox had told me. This was my Bobby. The one I loved. A guy sitting in his kitchen after a golf trip eating a sandwich. I tried to imagine this man before me in the flesh killing innocent children, and I couldn't. I simply couldn't.

From that moment on, I decided to just let this be my last days with him as we were. This was my husband, and I did love him. Nothing I had heard or seen took that feeling away when I stood in my front hallway and watched him living our lives as if nothing horrible existed or loomed on the horizon.

He looked up when he noticed me standing there and flashed that grin that always made me melt. He wiped his hands on a napkin and came over to hug and kiss me hello. After all that had happened, I melted. His arms, his chest, his smell, it just felt like home. It still felt right.

We went through out daily routine and made love before going to sleep. I knew it would be the last time, so I completely gave myself over to the fantasy that this was my husband, and there was nothing wrong. No lies, no raid happening, I wasn't about to walk away from my life and not know what the future was going to bring.

As I lay there drifting off to sleep, and listened to Bobby's breathing, I even toyed with the idea of telling him everything the FBI had planned for him, but I also knew I couldn't be the wife of a ruthless drug lord. This wasn't the mob where the wives kept house and got to wear nice clothes and drive nice cars even if their husbands had to 'go away' for a while every now and then. No protected sisterhood exists in that world. I didn't have the stomach for it.

My thoughts eventually put me to sleep, but I awoke a few hours later without Bobby next to me in bed.

"Bobby?" I called out into the darkness.

I got out of bed, and headed down the stairs, "Bobby? You up?"

When I reached the kitchen, I could see Bobby out on the deck talking on the phone, it looked like he was arguing with somebody. He was also speaking Spanish.

He didn't speak Spanish.

Well, my Bobby didn't, anyway.

I made my way towards the sliding glass door, and opened it. Bobby turned to face me, startled by the noise. This man wasn't my husband. This wasn't a stranger. His normally kind, big almond shaped brown eyes, were steely, and cold. His black hair wild from sleep. Shirtless, his tanned shoulders were tense and hunched with anger. Whatever was going on wasn't good.

"Ava, I'm just taking care of some business, go back to bed."

"At two a.m.?" I asked, "What kind of work crisis is getting you out of bed at two a.m.?"

I knew the answer to that, I really did. Now all of those fantasies I had been feeling were being wiped away by this anger bubbling up inside me. How many nights did I sleep through this? I wondered.

"Ava, I'll be right up," Bobby said again, not bothering to hide that this was a different man standing before me.

I stood there in the open doorway. I should just shut up and go back to bed, but my rage was consuming me at this point. The lie was right there staring me in the face, with God knows what order being carried out on the other end in Spanish.

Spanish.

Bobby doesn't speak Spanish.

"Spanish," I said holding his gaze, "You were speaking Spanish..."

"Ava," Bobby warned as he walked toward me, "Ava!"

I spun on my heel, running through the kitchen, down the hall and up the stairs. I was quick, but no match for Bobby. His stride alone made him faster than me. He tackled me face down on the stairs, smashing my right cheek into the carpeting. I could feel the each and every single fiber burning into my cheek. His knee fell with a jab into my lower back and I let out a scream. He flipped me over face up and put his hand around my throat, pushing the back of my head into the edge of the stair above me, and he straddled me with both legs.

His hand didn't tighten around my throat, and I think it would have had I not kept my stare locked on his. If he was going to kill me, he was going to have to remember my eyes on his.

He leaned over and whispered into my ear, "Go to bed, Ava. *Now*. I will be up in a minute."

Bobby stood up, released his hand from my throat, turned around and walked down the stairs. I heard him connect his call, and the sliding glass door click behind him as he went outside.

I went to the bathroom and looked in the mirror. The face looking back at me sported a cherry red rug burn on my cheek, a hand print around my neck, and a bruise starting on the curve of my lower back where he had stopped me with his knee. I opened the medicine cabinet and found a bottle of Percocet I had gotten when my wisdom teeth were pulled a couple of years ago. I never finished the medication, and still had half a bottle left. I popped open the cap and poured the pills into the palm of my hand. About ten.

Swallowed them. All. Didn't even need water. I threw the bottle in the trash can, turned off the light, and made my way to the bed. I pulled the covers to my chin, and lay my head on the pillow.

I couldn't do this. Why was this happening to me? God. Wasn't my childhood enough of a payment on some kind of cosmic debt? I had lost my parents, my sister for all intents and purposes, my passion and my surrogate family at the studio, and now my husband? What would be the point of going on? Starting all over again before the age of thirty? No. I had no fight left. I was tired.

I laid there and cried as I felt the warm haze of the drugs wash over me. I was happy, floating, free. Hopefully it would last forever.

But it didn't. Of course it didn't. I'm never that lucky.

CHAPTER 3

Wilcox didn't tell me when the raid would happen, but he told me how to prepare for it. I had my dance bag packed with what I wanted to take with me when it went down. That's it. One bag. Here I lived in a four bedroom house, had twenty seven years of life behind me, and I had to condense it all into one bag.

He told me not to worry about clothes or anything, because all of that would be handled once he got me to the safe house. The bag was for things like mementos, or things that couldn't be replaced. So I put things in there like my parents' wedding picture, my mother's jewelry, the necklace my teacher got for me after I graduated from Juilliard, and some other odds and ends not really worth mentioning.

There was something in me that wanted to find a way to contact my sister Maria and tell her what was going on. I don't know why, we weren't exactly close. When my father went away, we were separated and shipped off to different aunts and uncles. She wound up with Aunt Drea and Uncle Joe on the south side. We saw each other on the weekends and holidays, but by then we were so different, it was like seeing cousins or something. We still had our 'twin telepathy,' so it wasn't like we needed each other so much, but we just never became sisters in the true sense of the word.

I hadn't seen her in a few years, but I had a feeling she was in the 'family business' so to speak. Uncle Joey ran a bar that she eventually took over when he retired. However, she was a lot wealthier than you would expect out of a local neighborhood tavern owner. The last time I saw her, she rolled up in a new Mercedes and her purse probably cost more than a year's worth of rent on my studio.

Whereas I grew up a suburban princess, my Uncle Nick was a chemical engineer not at all connected to the 'family', and Maria was all mob. Tough, street smart, and nobody's fool. Uncle Joey didn't have any kids or a son to pass the family business down to, but Maria was eager to step into the role.

The bar was a front for money laundering...that was obvious. The 'coffee' business was always booming, and the bar gave a nice front to turn that money around. With Maria being as quick and smart as she was, she probably made it better than a nice front. She probably made the whole operation happen.

Even though she was good at what she did, I think she always resented that I ended up in a big house with a manicured lawn in the 'burbs, and she ended up where she did. I too, think it sucks that our family decided to separate us. While she got to be an only child, I suddenly had to be a seven year old finding my way and pecking order with three other kids. I became quiet and withdrawn, preferring my own company, while Maria managed to have the requisite sighing response when the Aunts would recount her exploits and all the trouble she managed to get herself into.

I guess my need for Maria was my need for someone. Anyone. I was completely alone in all of this because Wilcox told me that if I told a soul, that would be it. Everything would be compromised.

So here I sat in my closet, checking and rechecking my bag waiting for the three telltale signs it was going down.

The battering ram on the door.

The glass shattering in one of the downstairs windows as a teargas canister gets thrown in.

The eventual spray of gunfire.

That's what he told me to listen for. If I had happened to see something before then, a change in Bobby, his guys around the house, I should quietly take myself upstairs, grab my bag, and head to my designated hiding place, which was decided by Wilcox to be a small storage crawl space with a trap door that came out of the ceiling like an old attic hatch. He had me practice opening the door, pulling down the ladder, climbing it, and pulling the ladder back up so it would be easy for me when the time came. I spent an entire afternoon while Bobby was gone practicing the drill until my t-shirt and shorts were completely drenched in sweat.

The day after Bobby had pinned me to the stairs, I slept into late the afternoon with the help of the pills. I didn't die, because they made me so sick I wound up puking not long after I fell asleep. Bobby still hadn't come to bed, so he didn't have anything to be suspicious about. Luckily, I wasn't so far gone I didn't wake up when I got sick.

Drowning in my own vomit would have only added insult to injury at that point.

It could have been the drugs, it could have been emotional exhaustion, but I slept and slept and slept until the sun was low in the sky and the shadows were long. I slowly made my way downstairs, and went into the kitchen for a glass of water. Bobby was sitting on the couch watching a baseball game on the big screen like it was just another day. I could feel my anger bubbling up again, but the burning that still throbbed under the skin of my cheek and my sore neck prevented me from acting out on my impulses. I cleared my throat, grabbed a glass and filled it like any other time I would.

Hearing the noise in the kitchen, Bobby turned around on the couch and beamed at me, "Wow! You've never slept this late. You must have been exhausted! You feeling okay, honey?"

Like nothing at all had happened. Like I wasn't standing in the middle of our kitchen with a rug burn on my face and bruised on my neck he inflicted, sick after a botched suicide attempt. Yeah, I don't think I'm feeling very well today, Bobby.

"I'm okay," I croaked; frozen as I gaped at him, "Just getting a drink and I think I'll go lay back down."

"Okay," he said brightly, "Let me know if I can get you anything. I think I'm gonna go get takeout for dinner tonight. Sound good?"

"Yeah," I said absentmindedly. Out of the corner of my eye, I thought I saw something dart across the back lawn through the kitchen window. I smiled at Bobby, and he went back to his game, while I looked again to see if it was just a hallucination brought on by a handful of narcotics and a life circling the drain, or something else.

I saw another movement in the hedges that lined the left side of our back yard. And then another. Finally I saw what looked like the end of a sniper rifle poking through the branches of the evergreens.

SWAT. Had to be. They were here. It was time.

I set my glass on the counter, and slowly made my way out of the kitchen and up the stairs. I glanced up at the window as I climbed, and saw the cars and trucks closing in. Then I heard Bobby's phone ring.

Here we go.

My adrenaline completely kicked in at this point, as I sprinted up the remaining stairs, down the hall to our bedroom, and grabbed my bag. I heard the battering ram as I ran back down the hall and to the crawlspace. I pulled the cord, and like I had practiced, got the ladder down, climbed up, sat on the rafter and pulled the ladder up, clicking the trapdoor shut.

Even though I was basically in a wall, I could hear almost everything going down below me. Shouts, screams, gunfire. It seemed to go on forever until it was silent for a while. I sat there hugging my knees, shivering with fear and holding my breath until I heard the clicking of someone grabbing the cord to the trap door, and the squeaking of the hinges as it was was opened and the ladder was loaded.

"Ava," Wilcox said without any emotion.

"Y-y-yes?" I answered.

"Come out, follow me, and keep your eyes down. It's time to go."

"I don't have any shoes."

"We'll get you shoes. Let's go now."

I climbed down the ladder, my legs aching and stiff from being curled up shaking on the rafter the whole time, and Wilcox helped me down the last few rungs. His hands were like catcher's mitts. And again, I felt safe enough to trust this man with my life.

He put an arm around my shoulder and led me down the hall and back down the stairs, pulling me close as we made our way down, "Do not look around. Just watch your feet and walk out, alright?"

"Okay," I answered.

And I didn't look. I could smell the acrid scents of gunpowder, tear gas, and blood as I walked out my front door for the last time. Once outside, the late afternoon sun stung my eyes, and I saw the people of the neighborhood lined up on the street watching Mrs. Giancola get led out by an agent, and various body bags following her and paramedics running in with law enforcement helping the wounded. I wondered if Bobby was one of them as Wilcox helped me into the back of the dark sedan that was parked at the curb only a few days ago.

Once he was in the driver seat, I asked the obvious question, "Was Bobby killed?"

"No," he answered flatly.

"Oh," I said. I wasn't sure if I was relieved or not, "How many?"

"Four. Three wounded."

Seven. Seven people shot in my house. That will be the stuff of urban legends and tales for kids to tell as they walk past the house on the way to school for years to come.

"I'm sorry," I said quietly.

Wilcox met my gaze in the mirror, "For what?"

"If any agents died, or were injured, I'm sorry. That has to be hard," I answered.

Wilcox took a breath, "Well, we did lose two. Tactical guys I didn't know very well. Sorenson got clipped with a graze wound, but he should be okay. The rest were Bobby and his guys. Bobby got shot in the shoulder, but he should be fine. The other guys were just muscle, I'm sure."

I nodded my head and looked out the window while he drove. After about a minute I felt his eyes on me via the mirror again.

"So what's the deal with your face?" he asked.

I kept looking out the window, "The ladder hit me in the face when I pulled it down. I guess I should've practiced more."

His eyes left the mirror and went back on the road. We were silent for the rest of ride.

I have no idea why I lied to this man, currently the only person in the world I had.

But I did. Without even thinking or blinking, I straight up lied to him.

Looking back on that, I now realize it was my way of keeping something for myself. My whole life had been invaded, and I wanted some events to be mine and only mine. That moment on the stairs between Bobby and I, where any delusion I had harbored that my husband wasn't this horrible monster was rubbed out in the carpet on my right cheek, didn't belong to Wilcox or the United States Vs. Roberto Raul Perez. It belonged to me. Ava Giancola. The wife of a dead baby.

The truth was absurd.

The Secret Life of Lies

The lie made sense.

* * *

Wilcox walked back into the room with a fresh cup of piping hot coffee, and chose to stand leaning against the wall to continue their conversation. He told Ava he needed to use the restroom and get some coffee after she had recounted that part of the story, but the truth was he needed some air to compose himself. As she recounted what she went through, it dawned on him why things took the turn they did. Here was a woman who had already had her whole life uprooted once, had it happen again, and she had been completely innocent in all of it. You probably have a better chance of getting stuck by lightning. She had to walk away, and do it fast. No warning. No time to process any of it, and really no time to mourn. Wilcox had been on the job so long that he had completely forgotten how completely shattering this was for 'normal' people. Imagine what it must be like for someone just trying to find normal.

He could've taken the time to check out Ava Giancola to find out she was the Ava Santini who just happened to be a branch of the Santini-Lazaro family tree. He would have known about Maria, and who he was dealing with. No wonder she blamed him. All it took was one more step he was too quick to dismiss once he found out that the Ava Santini who married Bobby Giancola went to Our Lady of Perpetual Hope in the completely boring suburb of Geneva, IL, went on to the Juilliard, a short stint in the Joffery, then as principle dancer in the Pacific Ballet before getting married and opening her studio. No record.

Squeaky clean. They weren't after her anyway. They wanted Bobby.

He looked at the tiny body laying in the hospital bed before him. The Ava he had met on her doorstep, petite, perfect tan skin, long flowing brown hair, bright green eyes, beautiful smile with perfect teeth, was not this broken bird laying in the bed before him now with dyed blonde hair, too thin, and the hospital lighting casting a greenish glow on her now pale olive complexion.

Wilcox had been trying to save her, and yet he ruined her at the same time.

He felt the cold cement painted brick of the hospital wall on the back of his head as he stood there and watched Ava sleep while sipping his coffee. Not bad for hospital coffee, he thought to himself.

Ava sensing he was there, started to stir in her sleep and opened her eyes, not startled to see him standing there. She looked visibly uncomfortable.

"You all right? In a lot of pain?" He asked.

"Kind of, but I'm okay. It's not unbearable. I'm sure they'll give me another shot when they do rounds."

"You know, you never told me about Bobby attacking you, and I really get why you didn't."

"You do?"

Wilcox nodded his head and took a sip of coffee, "We can leave it unsaid. But I get it."

Ava nodded and closed her eyes, "You know, so many things were wrong then. I should have told you."

"Well," he shrugged, "I knew a lot of what you were hiding already, and just let it go, because it's normal to kind of go haywire in the head when something like this happens. Like when you went to visit Bobby. I knew about that and never said anything."

Ava raised her eyebrows and held his gaze.

"You think you're smarter than me? You think you're gonna outfox the FBI?"

CHAPTER 4

After the raid, we drove up north to Lake Tahoe and went through a lot of back roads until we reached a beautiful little cottage on the water. It wasn't the main channel, but a little lake that was pretty secluded except for an old trading post, and a boat rental place.

We had been silent most of the ride, as I stared out the window, still in shock, and let my mind go numb as the scenery blurred by. Occasionally, Wilcox needed a break and we got some snacks. We'd have a little small talk then, but it was pretty much silent. He listened to baseball and classic rock on the radio most of the way. It all sounded like white noise humming to me.

When we arrived at the cottage, it was late, and all I really wanted to do was fall into bed again and sleep forever. We were met by Agent Joy Garcia, a small and sturdy woman about my age who led me to my room and gave me the lay of the land, as well as what was going to happen from here.

The Secret Life of Lies

My room looked like a bedroom in a cabin. It was basic: a full sized bed, television, desk, chest of drawers, bookshelves with some dusty titles, a small bathroom off the far wall, it was comfortable, and where I would probably spend the first month or so. I couldn't stay in one place for too long, because Bobby's guys would find a way to get to me eventually.

There were clothes in my size and toiletries provided. The kitchen was stocked with food, and if there was anything I needed, I was to write it down and give it to Wilcox or Garcia. They would be staying with me for the duration. I would have to give a taped interview in the morning, and I was allowed to walk around the property, but I was not allowed to go on any main roads or into the town under any circumstances. And I was also not allowed to be near a phone. Garcia would call Renee to let her know I was safe and under the agency's protection.

"But what if I want to be done with all of this? What if I just say, 'fuck it' and want to go home to my life and take my chances?" I asked her.

Garcia furrowed her brows, "You mean no longer cooperate with the case?"

"No," I answered, "I mean, no longer want all of this protection. What if I wanted to see and talk to my friends and family, or go back to San Diego?"

With a sympathetic nod, Garcia's small brown eyes softened a bit, "You will die by the end of your first day. He will have you killed. Especially now that he knows you were cooperating with us."

"But I—"

"He knows. Trust and believe he knew it all. He will kill you for revenge. That's how it works."

She motioned for me to sit on the bed, "When I was in the academy, I was on a case similar to yours. The woman involved found out her husband, who she thought was just a local realtor selling houses in suburbia, was running guns for the Iranians into Afghanistan. Huge operation. He might have coached their son's little league team, but he was not a nice guy, and probably killed dozens of children by default, too."

I nodded, she probably sat in this room at one time. It was like the 'Cabin for tricked wives,' or something.

Garcia went on, "Much like you, she discovered the truth, and cooperated once she did. When the time came, she went into protective custody, and we kept her safe. Her sons were homeschooled through the agency, and we made sure to give them a pretty full life. But she had this pull to go home. This kind of isolation isn't for everybody. It drives people crazy sometimes."

"So what happened?" I asked.

"She went home, we couldn't stop her," Garcia answered.

"Did she die?"

"I have no idea. She disappeared within a day. Her boys were left behind. These guys are more into torture than killing. Whatever happened, it was probably horrible, and not at all worth going back. Now those kids are orphans."

I winced when she said that. I knew the feeling.

"It's going to be boring, you're going to be lonely, and once the shock wears off, you're going to have too many emotions you're not going to want to deal with among strangers, I'll do whatever you need. You need Xanax, I can get you some. You want to drink and cry? That's good too. You want to go shoot a gun? Great, I need the practice, but please, for the love of all things holy, please do not leave. Do not go back. It never, ever ends well."

I nodded and watched her leave the room. I sat there for a minute staring at the fading white paint that covered the wood paneling on the walls. So this is my life. A cabin in the woods with two FBI agent roommates I don't know. Well, I guess I can't ever complain about my life being boring, I guess.

I walked over to the chest of drawers, and opened them to find some sweats or something to change into. I was still wearing the clothes I had passed out in the night before. My mouth felt fuzzy and disgusting, and a hot shower would probably be life changing at this point. I just wanted this day to be over as soon as possible.

I selected a pair of black leggings and a white T-shirt, and the underwear that came in a bulk pack. There'd definitely be a note to Garcia in the morning, stating that since I was not a prisoner, prison issued underwear wouldn't be necessary.

I found a pair of flip flops on the floor of the closet, and slipped them on, then padded into the bathroom. The toiletries were a step up from the clothes, but not much. I opened the medicine cabinet to find the essentials plus some ibuprofen and night time cold medication. I tore into the box and grabbed two green capsules out of the blister pack of cold medicine. Grabbed a paper cup out of the dispenser, filled it with water from the tap, and washed them down with water that had a faint soil after taste.

The shower was above an old fashioned claw foot tub, and I smiled faintly at my unexpected luxury. At least I'd have baths. Lots and lots of baths. Hopefully I wouldn't find myself slitting my wrists and dying in this tub before it became too much.

I ran the water and got in the shower when it got good and hot. As soon as I got under the shower, the tears came. I stood there, my body wracking with sobs until the water ran cold.

I dried off, dressed and made my way to the bed. Climbed in the worn flannel sheets and the cold medicine carried me off to another dreamless sleep. Maybe I would wake up and this would be a dream. Maybe I would wake up to the smell of Wilcox singing Foghat horribly and frying eggs in his boxer shorts.

You guessed it. Scrambled eggs and 'Slow Ride' bright and early.

* * *

My first weeks at the cottage weren't all that horrible. I had my moments when things would start to sink in, like when it was time for formal interviews and meetings with lawyers, the DEA and other agencies.

Wilcox, who I started calling Dan after a few days, and I became pretty fast friends. He took me around the grounds and taught me about the woods and hiking the trails. There was a small ski boat docked at the lake, and he spent a lot of our days cruising around and fishing with me basically sitting there sunning myself because I was pretty useless at just about anything else. Once in a while, he would break the rules and sneak me off the property on his Harley and take us to McDonald's so I could get a break from our cooking. The only one that could cook was Garcia, and she was only there two days a week to relieve Wilcox so he could go take care of whatever personal life he might have.

And it really didn't sound like he had much of one besides his job. He was divorced and had a grown daughter and really kind of preferred the loner life of his job, riding his Harley, and just being a guy. He was going to retire after my case was over, and he was looking forward to spending the rest of his life on the beach and living on a boat.

"Living the Parrot Head dream, huh," I had teased him.

He put his hands over his head to mimic a shark fin, "Fins up!" Then he became thoughtful, "I've seen a lot on this job. There's something about it that just gets into your blood and it becomes all you are. I want to just blank the canvas a bit. Maybe looking at endless ocean will help me to let it go a bit, let me not be 'the job'."

"How did you even become an agent?" I asked, "If I met you under different circumstances, I would've had you pegged more Hell's Angels, not life long FBI agent."

"I was in the Navy. Went to 'Nam, did some intelligence work, and kind of liked it, so I went to the academy when I got home. Turns out, I'm really good at finding bad guys, and catching them. I hadn't really been good at anything else before. Well, maybe baseball, but I broke my femur in high school, so that took football out of the equation, and I really wasn't all that good at baseball, either."

I laughed. I really liked him. There was just something so comfortable and fatherly about him, I was drawn into everything he had to say. I know he was just doing his job, but I really felt safe and cared for when he was around. Garcia was great too, but there wasn't the kind of connection there I had with Wilcox. Some of my greatest memories are of those nights he would build a fire and we would split a six pack and talk about all kinds of things from life, the case, evolution, religion, politics, just about everything you could imagine. I think it kept me sane. Without him, I probably would have gone back home at some point.

I didn't obey him all the time, though. There was one thing I did that completely put all of us at risk.

* * *

Bobby sat shackled at the ankles and wrists in the visitation room. He leaned his elbows on the aluminum table and shifted his weight on the metal stool. Dark circles lined his eyes, and his stubble was filling in along his jawline. The bandage from his wound that was still healing peeked through the v neck of his prison scrubs. His hair was combed, but not neatly. He anxiously began to tap his toes when Agent Luke Johnston walked in the door.

Johnston, a young agent with clean cut quarterback good looks, tossed a file folder on the table and sat in the plastic chair on the other side of the aluminum table.

"You look like you've had better days," He laughed.

"You find her?" Bobby asked tersely, not at all amused by Johnston's light mood.

"No," Johnston said, "They've got your shit on lock, man. I can't find out anything. I know Wilcox is with her because they have to keep him out of sight right now, too.

But where? I have no idea. That's off the books and very close to the vest. And if I start asking around, it's only going to look suspicious."

Bobby's eyes burned with a building rage, "So what the fuck am I paying you for? I'm still in jail, the fucking bitch who put me here isn't dead yet, and you sit there like it's fucking funny."

Johnston stood up, "Man, I'm not sure what you expect me to do. You're not in here for some bullshit white collar crime. You killed federal agents in a shoot out, and you've been running cocaine through Central America into southern California for the last ten years. I'm not clear on how I'm supposed to get a guy facing multiple life terms back on the streets."

"You better find a fucking way or you're going to be dead, too," Bobby said through gritted teeth as the rage bubbled up inside him.

"It's going to be a while. There's too much media on this case right now. Let things die down a bit, go to trial, and just be as cool as you can. I'll make sure no one fucks with you in here and you'll get what you need to conduct business. Speaking of which," he pulled out a small package in his pocket and handed it to Bobby, "Stick that in your pants. Cell phone, charger, and some pain meds for your shoulder. I'll let the guard know I did the pat down before our interview so you should be good. Shove it up by your balls just to be on the safe side."

Bobby managed to get the package in his pants even though he was cuffed, while Johnston walked to the door. He grabbed the handle and met Bobby's still murderous stare.

"I'll keep working on finding her," he opened the door and called for the guard.

* * *

After a few weeks, it wasn't unusual for Wilcox and Garcia to leave me alone one day a week. I always just assumed they were going back to their lives, or sleeping in their own beds for a change, but I'm sure they were doing more FBI stuff. It seemed like the job never ended. There were more of me out there than I cared to think about.

I loved these days to myself. I would move the furniture in the small living room and dance until my feet hurt. Then I would cry. It felt good to cry. I felt the need to be brave in front of Wilcox and Garcia, and it felt weird to show emotion around them.

I always felt better after a good cry. It made it easier to accept my situation when I could grieve it. Grieve for my life and the things I had lost. But when I did it on this particular day, I was consumed with an overwhelming anger. Rage, even. I was in *prison*. Sure it was a picturesque view and a cozy little cottage, but I wasn't allowed to leave. I had to have someone else buy my tampons and groceries. My only meal out in the world was from a drive thru and it tasted like steak and lobster, because I had all but forgotten the outside world and craved the little excursions Wilcox provided.

But what had I done to deserve losing my entire life as I knew it? Nothing. I was a good wife. I am a good person. I did the right thing. I turned him in. And how was I rewarded?

The Secret Life of Lies

With prison. This prison. Because I trusted the man I loved to be who he said he was.

I'm the victim in all of this, and I'm the one being punished.

I sent a book end sailing across the room and it dented the paneling of the wall.

I was losing my mind.

I had to see Bobby.

For no reason than to look him in the eye now that the truth was out. And to also ask him why. Why me? Why bring me into all of this? He could have just been a bachelor. Did he ever love me? Where did bad Bobby end and good Bobby begin?

Why.

I knew that he was being held before his trial in the Metropolitan lockup in downtown Los Angeles. There was a small netbook I was allowed to have on the counter, and I quickly opened it to see the visitation schedule.

Visitation was scheduled for today, beginning at noon. It wasn't even 10am yet. It would take me just under eight hours to get there, so that would leave me with an hour to see him.

I had no car and no money so I had to think of how I was going to get there and back. Thumbing a ride seemed reckless. I know. I'm about to go AWOL from protective custody to visit my killer husband, and I am against hitchhiking. Clearly I was insane.

The boat rental place! There was a couple of dusty Ford Broncos they used to shuttle vacationers from the cabins to the lake with. I would run up there and ask if I could borrow one of their trucks. Perfect. Now all I needed was cash.

Jennifer Gulbrandsen

I started going through every jar and canister in the kitchen looking for a stash of cash. Everyone keeps a stash in the kitchen, even the FBI. And lo and behold, there it was. Tucked in a box of tea bags in the back of the cabinet were two one hundred dollar bills. So old they were not the new design. I guess mad money isn't used very often in a safe house. There's a thought.

I ran to my bedroom and threw on some clothes, not even bothering to shower, then I was off to the boat rental shack to see a guy about borrowing a car. I would make up some kind of story about a family emergency in L.A. I would have the Bronco back by the next morning.

Another lie. They seemed to be getting easier.

* * *

If someone asked Maria Santini if she was Ava Giancola, the woman on the news, one more time, she was going to scream. She was at the store this morning when this little old lady asked her, and she was so annoyed, she told the woman to fuck off. That's one for the confessional later.

The media was relentless in their coverage of the case, and why wouldn't they be? Here's this beautiful ballerina in her picture perfect marriage to a guy who built strip malls, finds out he's a drug czar? It was something right out of a miniseries. And unfortunately, Maria just happened to be that beautiful ballerina's twin sister. Only with a few more tattoos, pounds, and an attitude problem.

Maria found out about her sister's troubles like most people did, on the news. She was placing the bar's alcohol order and counting the bottles of Kettle One when she saw her sister's picture, her driver's license picture to be exact, flash in the mirror. Maria flew around the bar and ran to turn up the TV.

Her entire body went numb from shock as she heard the anchor prattle on about Bobby. She had only met Bobby twice since he always managed to be out of town when she would visit Ava in California, and he seemed like an incredibly boring and bland guy. Perfect for her sister. Now she was listening as an anchor on the news went on about how he was one of the most elusive and notorious dug lords of the modern era.

"Holy shit, she married Tony Montana," she whispered to herself letting out a sardonic chuckle. Maria wouldn't have been able to predict that in a million years. Even though she and Ava weren't exactly 'close,' especially being twin sisters, she still felt like she had that sixth sense where she could feel whether or not Ava was ok.

Her stomach sank as the story ended and they cut to some smarmy human interest story about a polar bear at the zoo painting portraits. She was such a piece of shit sister. Here Ava was in serious danger for all these years, and Maria was basically absent from her life beyond the occasional phone call and birthday card. She should have known something was going on. After all, it's not like Maria was living the life of a church mouse and cleaning the rectory for a living.

Ava got out and moved across the country while Maria stayed behind. After the whole tortured adolescence thing, she did try to go off to college and become a respectable contributor to society. She enrolled in one of the city colleges and decided she would try her hand at psychology. Why not? If she could get through her whole life to that minute without committing a homicide, maybe she had some sanity to offer the world.

She was an average student, but there was something really lacking in the whole campus life thing. She hated most of the people there, found her professors to be mostly pontificating on academia rather than teaching anything useful to actually living a real life, and after two semesters, she found herself in this bar talking to one of her uncles, Angelo.

Angelo Santini was Salvatore's younger brother and much deeper in 'the family' than Sal ever was. Some say that Angelo set Sal up to take his fall so Angelo could have the heat off of him and move up in the ranks. Maria believed it to be true, because with the Santinis, any level of cloak and dagger treachery was possible, but she didn't hold it against him. She liked her Uncle Angelo and always secretly hoped he would have taken her in when her father went away. She understood him, he understood her, and he was one of the few people in the world she felt comfortable enough to be around.

That day in the bar, she told Angelo she was done with school and that she wanted to work for him.

"You? You don't want to find a nice boy to marry and settle down? How come? You're gorgeous, have all that moxy like your mother, and you would make someone a very happy man. I mean, look at Ava! She's found herself a good Italian boy and she's happy in sunny San Diego. You could have the same thing, you know. Why work in this shithole?"

"Because I'm not Ava. And this shithole makes me happy."

The Secret Life of Lies

Uncle Angelo laughed at this. His niece was a smart girl.

The Lorello family was the main mafia family in Chicago for a couple of generations. As the Lorello men were killed off or 'went away,' the Santinis started to become the family running the business. Uncle Angelo, Uncle Bambini (the youngest Santini boy), and their various sons, nephews and cousins began to take over the daily operations and created quite the modern organized crime empire. Maria would watch the meetings from a dark corner of the game room when she was little as they played cards and talked shop, and that was all the education she needed. She wanted to play with the big boys.

After some convincing, Maria became the manager of the Ruby Pub. Even though it was known as the 'shithole' in a family with banquet halls, steak houses, social clubs and family restaurants as fronts for their shadier business, the Ruby was a clean, dimly lit corner bar in one of the oldest Irish/Italian neighborhoods in the city. Clientele was typically blue collar and everyone knew everyone. Regulars had their own behinds worn into the barstools, and the conversations would range from how the White Sox were doing, how bad the Bears offense was last Sunday, to the occasional political debate. It was a nice family atmosphere that Maria loved and felt perfectly comfortable working in. Even if it was a front for a little money laundering.

It should have bothered her, but it really didn't. In her mind, everything had its place in the world. As far as she was concerned, she ran an honest business that may have a shady investor. As the old proverb went, not her circus, not her monkeys. Her Uncle Angelo had always been good to her and Ava, they never wanted for anything, and if there were bad things happening, it was usually deserved. Unfortunately, when you double cross the wrong people, bad things can happen.

Still in shock from the news, Maria made her way to her office and picked up her phone. Ava was the first contact on her phone, so she texted her.

Ava it's me. I just saw the news. Let me know you're ok.

As she waited for a response back, she flipped open her laptop and waited for it to boot up. Maria knew enough to know that a response from the Ava with the feds involved was probably not going to happen. Chances are they had her holed up in a safe house and she wouldn't be allowed to talk to anybody because even the mafia doesn't mess around with the Central American drug cartel thugs. Those guys don't mess around no matter who you are or who you're related to.

Still no response from Ava, so once the computer booted up, Maria put the name of Ava's dance studio in the search engine. She knew Renee was probably one of Ava's closest friends, if not *the* closest, and there was a chance she would have some information as to where Ava might be, or at least have some clue as to what was going on.

The phone rang three times before Renee answered.

"Renee?"

"Speaking. Who's this? Ava? Ava! Is that you? Oh my god!"

"No, no this isn't Ava. It's her sister, Maria. We met the last time I was out there. I was actually calling you to see if you had any idea what's going on with Ava right now."

Renee then told Maria about what had happened after Ava's meeting with Wilcox, and what had happened after the raid.

"That Wilcox guy showed up here the next day with the new keys to the locks. I didn't even know they had changed the locks until I showed up here and couldn't get in. I also didn't know I had a security detail following me for days before this happened, and I've been having one follow me since."

A knot formed in Maria's stomach, "This Wilcox guy ask you a ton of questions? Like about Ava's family or anything?"

"No, not at all," Renee answered, "He just handed me a manila folder with all of the real estate transfers handled, making the studio mine, and a check for half a year of operating expenses since business would probably take a hit when our director's picture hit the national news. But actually, we've been fine. Everyone knows what a good person Ava is. Nobody believes she had any idea Bobby was this awful criminal."

"I certainly didn't have any idea," Maria said, "I thought he was just some boring real estate guy in a polo shirt and khaki's. Certainly makes me think differently of drug lords, that's for sure. I can't believe they didn't ask about Ava's family, I mean, you would think they would want to keep us safe if there's a bunch of thugs looking for revenge while their leader is staring at a concrete wall in an orange jumpsuit."

"Yeah, that is odd, but I didn't think about that too much, it all happened so fast. I'm still in shock and I can't even believe it's real. I'm half expecting Ava to walk through the door right now."

Maybe it was the power of suggestion, but when Renee said that, Maria looked at her office door expecting Ava to walk through at that moment. A chill went up her spine and the knot in her stomach tightened.

"Renee, thanks so much. This has to be hard on you. Please call me at this number if you need anything, and I'll let you know if I hear anything on my end, okay?"

"Sounds good, I just hope she's being taken care of. Thanks for calling, Maria."

Maria ended the call and stared blankly at her computer screen. Then she dialed Uncle Angelo's number.

* * *

I was in the Bronco and on the highway faster than I thought I'd be. I still didn't have a plan as to how I would get in to see Bobby, but this force was pulling me south, and it was out of control at this point. Maybe I didn't even want to see Bobby, maybe I just wanted out of my little prison and control over my life again. I had that anxious need to flee building up in my system that made me leave Chicago the first chance I got.

I thought about a lot on that drive. I thought about my mother, my father, Maria, the aunts and uncles who raised us, dance, everything. Mostly I thought about Bobby. Was he that good, or was I that stupid? Or both? I mean, I was no stranger to organized crime. Even the people in my family who weren't 'connected' were *connected*. I was probably connected. Hell, I would probably bring down the whole Santini family at this point with all of the prying that must be going on into my past right now. Wilcox or Garcia hadn't asked me about anything except whether my parents were still alive and whether or not I had any siblings or other family that Bobby might go after. I said, "no" because I really didn't think he would go after anyone in Chicago. I had run from that life and wasn't at all connected to any of them anymore, except Maria.

But how did he pull it off? He was out of town, a lot. Was I naive that there was something other than work behind that? I never saw a father at the dance studio. Fathers signed tuition checks and took pictures at recitals. I never even thought of my student's fathers. Maybe I had just become accustomed to men never really being there. After all, where was my father?

That feeling of wanting to flee, see Bobby in the flesh, and have some kind of answers consumed me. Wilcox and Garcia did their best to tell me that I wasn't alone in all of this. Wives are duped every single day. The only thing I was guilty of was trusting the wrong man… who stole the identity of a dead baby and went on to kill children. Seeing that photo of the family he murdered or had murdered in my mind's eye still made me sick.

At least playing mind games with myself and meticulously dissecting every single moment of my life over the last five years made the 8 hour drive go fast. Before I knew it, I was pulling into the Metropolitan Federal Building and looking for a spot to park in inside the garage. I found a spot on the fifth level, and swung the wide body of the Bronco in to the space, put the truck in park and stared at the wall ahead of me with the engine running. My heart was going a million miles a minute and I wasn't even sure what I was going to do. I had no contingency plan about reporters or being recognized. I had no idea if I would get in trouble for leaving the safe house, I had no idea if they would even let me see Bobby anymore.

My trance was broken by a knock on the glass. I startled and screamed. A tall man in a suit, flashed a badge in the window and told me to roll it down.

"The hell are you doing here?" he asked, not so nicely.

Sticking my head slightly out the window, I got a better look at him. He looked like he played football at a college in the middle of a cornfield. All the agents sort of looked like this with the exception of Sorenson and Wilcox; it was somewhat of a phenomenon, I thought. Send all your large, clean cut, farmboys to the FBI.

Seeing him did nothing for the heart attack I was having already in progress. But the theme of my panic was now not what am I going to do, but oh shit I just got caught.

"I'm here to visit my husband," I sputtered out once I got my tongue unstuck from the roof of my mouth, "He's in custody."

"Wilcox know where you're at?" he again asked tersely.

Hmmm…trick question. Had I been caught? Or was this a set up?

"Um…," I started, not sure of how to answer him.

"You aren't supposed to be here. You know you aren't supposed to be here," he interrupted, "Get out of the car," he commanded.

The Secret Life of Lies

"What? Am I under arrest?" I asked, "I don't even know who you are."

"Which is why you shouldn't leave a safe house because I could be anybody. I'm Agent Johnston. Now get out of the car."

I did what he said, stepping down from the Bronco onto the pavement, feeling the hot sticky air of the summer afternoon in the parking garage. Johnston immediately grabbed me by the arm and swung me around.

"Walk," he said leading me to a back stairwell.

He's right. This is exactly why you don't leave a safe house. Because at this moment, I could tell that I was anything but safe.

CHAPTER 5

Johnston led me down the back stairway and through a series of tunnels that I assumed went underground and we ended up in the Federal Building in some back stairwell. He buzzed us through with his keycard and led me down another hallway. It was stark, gray and very institutional, so I figured we were somewhere near the jail and this was some kind of transport route for prisoners.

"Am I in some kind of trouble?" I asked.

"Should I have brought you in through the front where a reporter would see you? Your face has been on every national news outlet every fifteen minutes. I think they're already making a Lifetime movie about you," he answered leading me through this impossibly long hallway that finally ended at an elevator. He used a key to call it, and pushed me on, then punched the key to the floor we were heading to. B9.

The doors of the elevator opened to reveal another hallway of brightly lit rooms with one small window each. The rooms were obviously locked from the outside and each small room had a metal table and stool, both bolted to the floor, and another chair with a back on the other end of the table. Interview rooms. I was probably about to be interrogated. And of course they would interrogate me. I had just left a safe house, and drove 8 hours to see the man who effectively ruined my life without much fear of being killed in the process. If they weren't going to interrogate me, they were going to probably commit me.

He opened one of the rooms and shoved me in.

"Sit," he said. Then the door slammed and locked behind me.

***

I sat there and stared out the window of the room into the hallway for what seemed like and eternity. No one came down the hallway, I heard no doors open and close. All sorts of scenarios were playing through my head when I finally heard a door open and close with that jailhouse metallic thud down the hall. Then I heard chains dragging on the ground.

I stood up and pressed my face against the window to see down the hall, and there he was. Bobby. Led by the arm by Agent Johnston, shackled and shuffling down the hall. I immediately became terrified and regretted this whole plan. Something about physically seeing him, remembering what he did to me before the raid, and the hate in his eyes, made me want to beat on the glass and scream my lungs off. I did not have a good feeling about this at all.

And it turns out I was right.

I was shaking so hard my molars were about to shatter when I heard Johnston slip the key into the lock and open the door. He gave me a cold stare as he entered and Bobby shuffled in behind him.

He told Bobby to go into the corner and face the wall, and when he did, he produced a set of cuff keys and undid all of Bobby's restraints. I could see a bandage on his shoulder sticking out of the neck of his prison scrubs, where he had been hit by a bullet in the raid. Johnston motioned to him to take a seat on the stool, and pointed to the chair for me to sit in. He then stood at the door facing us with his arms folded across his chest.

Bobby looked me up and down and sneered like a jackal coming across a fresh carcass after the lions had left. The metallic taste of fear had replaced my dry mouth, and I wanted to run out the door and never, ever look back. I looked over my shoulder at Johnston and he just continued to look of into the cement wall stone faced.

"Ava, Ava, Ava," Bobby taunted, "Why are you here? I wasn't prepared for a conjugal visit so soon. Maybe you shouldn't have dropped that dime on me so quickly."

"I didn't drop a dime on you," I answered, my eyes meeting his, "You lied to me. You killed children. My life was the one ruined here. I'm also in prison. I can't eat, I can't sleep, I can't do anything without someone watching me."

"Awww…poor Ava. You can't do anything except drive here to see me, apparently completely free to do so. I bet you didn't get a day pass for that," Bobby leaned forward and put his elbows on the table, "So why all the trouble to come see me, mi amor? Miss me? Want to say you're sorry? Want to go back to your nice, quiet life where all you had to do was be happy?"

The Secret Life of Lies

"No," I answered, "I just want to know why. Why me? Why did you pick me? Did you even love me to do this to me?"

He was out of that stool and had me picked up and thrown against the brick wall before I could even get the last word of my sentence out and take another breath. The back of my head taking the brunt of the impact and my skull felt like it was being seared with a flame thrower.

Johnston didn't flinch except to say, "Don't hit her in the face. I'm not doing the paperwork."

Bobby held me against the wall with the side of his body and his left hand around my throat. Obviously the shoulder injury took him out of commission, but even with his weaker hand, I could feel the oxygen leaving my body and black spots forming in front of my eyes.

"Don't kill her either, Bobby," Johnston said from what felt like light years away.

Bobby released his grip from my neck and as I was sliding down the wall he punched me in the stomach causing whatever air I had left to leave my body. As I lay on the floor gasping for air and choking, I felt a swift kick to the kidneys that almost made me black out.

Bobby kneeled down next to me and whispered in my ear, "You're dead. One day, I'm going to be there. And you're going to be dead. It will be slow. It will hurt. And I will enjoy the shit out of it."

I closed my eyes so I wouldn't have to see his eyes anymore. They almost glowed red with rage, and cut to my very core. I heard Johnston say something like, "That's enough. We're done," as the shackles got reapplied, but I was slipping out of consciousness. The last thing I remember was the thud of the steel door and hearing the chains drag down the hall again.

And then everything went dark.

* * *

I woke to a bottle of water being poured on my head.

"Get up," Johnston said.

I slid myself into a sitting position propped up against the wall. The light burned my eyes and it hurt every time I took a breath. Johnston handed me the remnants of the bottle of water he had poured on my head and handed me a couple of pills.

"You're breathing and you can see, so take those and I'll take you back out to the car so you can get back to wherever you are being held. I'm not going to ask you where that is, because it won't be hard to figure out. It's obviously in California if you made it here without fear of being caught. I'm also not worried about you keeping your little visit a secret, because I'm sure you enjoy your federal protection and don't feel to great about the idea of being tortured to death on your husband's orders. So get up, and let's get your happy ass out of here."

I really don't remember anything else after that point except waking up in my bed the next morning back in Lake Tahoe.

* * *

"We were out of there the next day," Ava remembered, smiling at Wilcox.

"Yep. That was no easy feat either. I had to come up with a reason to move you to Oklahoma City that didn't make me look like a complete asshole."

"How'd you find out?" she asked.

"I came back up to the house and you were gone. I walked around town asking about you and the kid at the boat rental place said you borrowed one of the Broncos for the day and had planned to bring it back that night. I also noticed the money missing from the stash, and I knew you went down to L.A. to see Bobby. You are not atypical of a victim who wants to see the person responsible for their pain. That's a normal thing. Stupid, but normal," Wilcox took a sip of his coffee and continued, "You also slept for 18 full hours. Had I known then what I know now, I think things would've been different. I always had a hinky feeling about that Johnston guy, but I could never quite place what it was."

Ava laughed, "Hinky. Like Scooby Doo. I can think of a lot of ways to describe Luke Johnston, and 'hinky' isn't one of them."

Wilcox shrugged, "There are a lot of guys who get into the FBI and they want to be right-fighting cowboys. Truth, honor, and the American way and all that. Never cracked open a book in their lives, but they can tell you every word of an Academy textbook from memory. This kid seemed really eager to know what I knew about the case. He was very interested in you and your role, how I was hiding you, and how it was eventually going to end," he took another sip of coffee, wincing at the taste of the final dregs, "I guess we now know why, huh. Super Agent was on the take. Didn't see that coming."

He pitched the cup into the waste basket and reached for his coat, "Listen, kiddo, it's been a long day and I have some work to get done. Why don't you take a break and rest and we'll pick this up again tomorrow. We can reminisce about our time in Oklahoma. Remember when I took you to the rodeo?"

Ava smiled, "Yeah, it smelled."

Wilcox smiled back, "Yeah, it kind of did, but it was a good year anyway," he put his coat on and headed for the door, "Take care, we'll pick this up tomorrow."

Ava closed her eyes and remembered the long drive from Lake Tahoe to Oklahoma City. She drifted off to sleep remembering that leg of her journey.

"I guess it really was a good year," she thought to herself.

* * *

Angelo Santini sat there looking at his niece through his highball in 'his booth' at the pub, "No. We can't, Maria. We're freaking lucky that we don't have a gaggle of feds on our front doorstep right now. Hell, this place is probably bugged and they're just sitting there in the car waiting to pounce," he paused to drain his glass. "Fuck."

Maria refilled the glass with Johnny Walker. Angelo wasn't much of a drinker beyond Chianti, but he did hit the hard stuff when he was stressed. This was obviously one of those times.

"Don't worry, Tio," Maria said, "Ava's got the 'good girl theory' going for her right now."

"The what?"

"The good girl theory," Maria answered pouring herself a glass, "When one of the guys here goes down, nobody bothers the wife, right? They watch her for a day, run her name through LEEDS, and if nothing flags, she's not really worth their time except to maybe get some info from her, right? She's a good witness, a law abiding citizen, and if they dig too deep, they might find some skeletons in her closet and then that good witness becomes shit. So, in Ava's case, they did all of that, she was in the Joffery before the internet got hot and heavy so all of that press wouldn't even come up on a Google search, so to them she's just a good girl that got caught up with a bad guy. That's what they need, so that's what they're going to do. Bobby's lawyer could bring it all up at trial, but probably won't because the last thing the Perez family needs is a bunch of pissed up paisanos vacationing in Costa Rica, am I right?" she raised her glass and they toasted.

Maria looked down at the table and said softly, "She's family, Angelo. She's my sister. My twin sister."

Angelo's eyes welled up with tears, "I know Maria. I know. But she's the FBIs right now. We get into that mix, it's like telling them to come over for dinner and look at the books."

"Or it has the opposite effect because we're kind of hiding in plain sight."

Angelo grumbled and sucked down the drink, slamming his glass onto the table making Maria jump.

"We wait," he commanded, "They wouldn't let us talk to her anyway because I'm sure Bobby's got eyes on us by now to see if any of us are jumping. Maria, look at me."

Maria looked up and met his watery gaze.

Jennifer Gulbrandsen

"We. Wait."

***

"So, you told me Ava's family are mob, right? Coffee importers?" Johnston asked Bobby in the interrogation room.

"Yes, my guy Hector has been watching them for a while, old family, old business," Bobby answered.

"Yeah, Bobby, old being the operative word. You know the supposed crime boss is like, 70, right? And every one underneath him is also about to check in to Shady Acres Rest Home. Maybe they get some city projects here and there and grease few local government palms, but these are not the big time mafioso you think they are. We barely have a file on them, and that's almost two decades old. Small time. And they haven't done a thing to ask about Ava as far as I know, and there has been no movement from any of them to go anywhere outside the ordinary with them. No flights here, no road trips. Everyone is living like it's just another day in Chicago."

Bobby was getting agitated by Johnston's response. Hector was one of his best intel guys and had been watching the Santini family for a couple of years now. Bobby's idea being that he could somehow infiltrate their coffee exporting operations to open up another pipeline north for himself. These were not little small time guys. These guys would pose a big problem if they got pissed off enough. They also had people on the inside that would make Bobby's life a living hell with one phone call. How did the FBI find out about him but not know the Santinis were a big deal?

The Secret Life of Lies

"Listen man, I'm telling you, the Santinis are going to make this difficult. Hector is one of the best, and if he tells me, it's true. You better get a little sharper at earning that government paycheck," Bobby said tersely.

"I don't have to do shit for you, Bobby. I tell you what I know."

"You're right, Johnston, you don't have to do shit for me, but you like the money. I'm sure Katie and your kids, what are their names? Leo and Kayla? Yeah, I'm sure they like it when Daddy can take them to see Mickey and I'm sure they like their nice house in Encino. It would be a shame if any of that changed."

Johnston slammed his hands on the table and leaned into Bobby's face, "You had better not be threatening my family. You had better not fucking ever touch my family. I will kill you myself."

Bobby laughed in his face, "Who said anything about killing anyone? All I said is it would be a shame if any of that changed because you weren't very good at your job. So maybe you should get better at it. Like find out where Ava is, or get me out of here. People escape all the time, you know."

Johnston stood up and turned around to compose himself. He then turned back around to face Bobby who was still smiling as if they were talking about pleasant things like the weather, "I'll work on finding out where Ava is. They moved her the day after she was here, so I don't know if she told them what happened and they're just waiting for us to screw up, or if somehow Wilcox is playing us just for fun and knows something is up. I guess we'll find out soon enough. And you're not escaping. The manhunt would be so intense, they would pull every single camera in this place, every phone call, every letter in code, and my ass would be the first all over the media and torched. Fuck that. You're going to hang tight here until your trial, get found guilty, and then we'll have a judge overturn your sentence on a technicality. That's the plan. So sit tight, mi amigo. Revenge will be sweeter the longer you wait."

"Definitely," Bobby said still smiling.

* * *

Garcia didn't talk to me unless she had to when we left Lake Tahoe. I could sense she was angry about having to move from this safe house so abruptly. She told me from the beginning that we would probably move a few times, and we wouldn't always have notice, but this seemed different. It seemed personal.

I was moving rather gingerly since returning back from my visit with Bobby, and I made sure to be covered from wrists to ankles at all times because I didn't want Wilcox or Garcia to see my bruises. There was a knot on my head that was so tender, I could hardly wash my hair without blinding pain. I probably had a concussion, but since I was still alive I ruled out any lasting internal damage.

"Will you hurry up!" Garcia snapped at me, "Wilcox wants us at the handoff before noon!"

"Where's that?" I asked.

"That's not for you to know, Giancola. Pick up the pace or we're going to be late."

Giancola. That was the first time I had heard that name in a couple of months, now. In my mind, I was just 'Ava' at this point. Giancola was a pretend name that belonged to a dead baby anyway. It certainly wasn't mine anymore.

"Garcia, what's wrong?" I asked.

Garcia's face softened for a second as she looked at me. So it was personal. I had done something to upset her.

"It's my son's first day of first grade and I'm missing it," she said, her eyes welling up with tears, "I was supposed to be there, but with this unscheduled move, here I am, gone for two days and missing all of it."

Oh god. I felt terrible, "I'm so sorry. But there will be so many more first days of school to celebrate."

Garcia got a dark look in her eye, "Oh will there, Ava? Will there be more first days of school? You're sure of this? You're sure that cases won't get compromised, and witnesses won't decide that they need, 'one last look' and I'll actually get this day back?"

"I said I was sorry," I stammered, "I didn't mean—"

"You didn't mean *what* Giancola? What. I told you those stories of what could happen for a reason, didn't I?"

My stomach dropped to my feet and I almost fainted, I had been found out. Shit.

"So what are you saying? Am I going to another safe house or is something else going on?"

"I told you to hurry up, is what I said. Now hurry up and get your crap in the car. We need to get going. Just remember that the operative word in safe house, is *safe*."

I didn't know what to make of that whole exchange, and from then until the last time I saw her after the trial, Garcia called me, "Giancola," which made the hair on my neck stand up, and treated me rather bruskly. Which I could understand now that instead of being just hours away from her family, she was now states away.

Jennifer Gulbrandsen

We took mostly back roads on our way south and the landscape was beautiful as the sun came over the mountains as dawn broke. We would be meeting Wilcox for the handoff in about six hours, and since we were heading south, I imagined that would be somewhere in Nevada. Since my life had become a horrible crime novel, I figured this would happen somewhere in the middle of a desert with a tumbleweed being blown across the highway as I got out of Garcia's cruiser and got into Wilcox's car.

I had grabbed a couple of magazines and books on my way out of the cabin and spent my time escaping into the lives of celebrities I didn't know, reading a couple of articles about myself, my favorite being "The Ballerina and The Bad Boy," in a gossip rag that only got about 4% of the facts right, including a picture of a Santini family in Chicago that I had never met, but were supposedly my family. But mostly I just zoned out on the open landscape and let my mind rest. Every now and then I would see Bobby's face in that interview room and my heart would jump at the memory. I was still so puzzled and conflicted with the feelings of how a man who loved me so much and was so gentle and kind, could be the monster that would have killed me with his bare hands if Agent Johnston had been more motivated to check off 'oops' on his incident report. All those years were a total lie. I was his front to a legitimate cover life that would remove him from suspicion.

Yeah, about that. The way Wilcox described it, they had their eye on Bobby since he was born, but that couldn't have possibly been the case if he flew under the radar for so long. He basically lived in America his whole life, assimilated, and became adept at living a double life while no one was watching the scion of the Perez family who would one day inherit the business? Nothing about this remotely made sense to me. The truth was so much stranger than fiction in all of this.

I made a mental note to ask Wilcox about this on our drive to wherever it was we were going, and tried to busy my mind with other things. I thought about dance and how my life may have been different if I had just stayed at the Joffery. The need to run hadn't worked out so well for me, huh. Character flaw, I guess. That and being ridiculously naive.

I must have drifted off to sleep because I startled myself awake when the car came to a sudden stop outside a small diner just off the highway. It was the quintessential greasy spoon right down to the neon sign that said, "Dottie's." I wondered if there would be a cook named Mel and sassy waitresses in pink dresses. Of course Wilcox would pick a place like this. It was so…*Wilcox*.

"We're here," Garcia barked.

"Oh good. I'm starving."

"No, Giancola, you don't get to go in. Tell me what you want, and I'll get it to go."

"How am I supposed to know what to order if I don't see a menu?" I asked.

I could see Garcia roll her eyes in the rear-view mirror, "Jesus. You're at a road side diner in the middle of nowhere. What the hell do you think is on their menu, a crown roast? Eggs, short stacks, burgers, maybe a Monte Cristo if you're lucky. So what do you want?"

"I guess I'll have a burger and fries with a coke," I answered sheepishly. I really wanted pancakes, but I didn't think eating cold rubbery pancakes in the back of Wilcox's car was the meal I was hoping for."

"Stay here, don't move, Wilcox will be out in a minute," she tossed a plain black baseball cap on me, "put this on and make sure your hair is tucked up inside."

A few minutes later Wilcox sauntered over to Garcia's cruiser looking nonchalant in his weathered jeans, motorcycle jacket, and boots. He motioned over to a van parked in the corner of the lot under a tree, and I groaned upon seeing it. It was a Chester van. You know what I'm talking about, the kind of van you were warned never to go near as a kid? Especially if they were offering you candy? Yeah, brown metallic paint with some kind of Native American goddess airbrushed on the side guided by wolves and eagles. Wilcox must've seen my reaction through the window because he was laughing as he opened my door.

"Got some leg room for the rest of the trip, isn't it great?" he giggled.

"Yeah, if we're killing some hookers on our way to wherever, or smoking tons of pot with our band mates," I said getting out of the car and following him over to the van.

"Oh you say that now, Ava, but once you spend an hour in this vinyl covered luxury, you aren't ever going to want to go back to life in the back seat of a cruiser. It's even got a mini fridge, man!"

Holy hell, he was like a kid in a candy store. I wondered whether I was Cheech or Chong. Something Wilcox found hilarious, apparently because he laughed for a full three minutes while we waited inside the van for Garcia to bring my food.

The Secret Life of Lies

Garcia briskly walked out of the restaurant and toward the van with a take out bag in her hand, and her permafrown on her face that hadn't moved since Lake Tahoe. Poor Garcia. I really did feel bad for her. She handed me the bag through the open side door where I was sitting on the bench seat, without looking at me, and slid the door closed after handing me the bag without a word. She went up to the driver's seat where Wilcox was now sitting, and had a few quiet words with him I couldn't hear. I tore into my meal, because I was starving at this point, and left them to their business while I ate a hamburger in the back of a van with shag carpeting and curtains with fuzzy ball tassels. This was my life now. You had to laugh or you would cry.

Wilcox and Garcia must have said their goodbyes, because I was jolted out of my shag carpeting trance by the roar of the engine turning over.

"Hear that, Ava?" Wilcox yelled over the engine, "This baby is full of nothing but power! Wahoo!" he gleefully cheered as he backed out of the parking space. With spinning tires and a cloud of dust, we were on our way to wherever I was going next.

CHAPTER 6

"So when do you tell me where we're going?" I asked Wilcox as we traversed what felt like endless miles of desert. I had moved from the shag carpeted back end of the van up to the passenger seat next to him. We chatted about nothing, but enjoyed the silence with each other for the most part.

"You ever been to Oklahoma?" He asked me.

Had I ever been to Oklahoma? I thought to myself for a second. My lifetime now felt like centuries instead of just 27 years.

"No, I don't think I've ever been to Oklahoma," I answered, "Why, is that where we're going?"

"Yep, we're going to a ranch just outside Oklahoma City. No animals or anything fun like that, but you'll have a lot more space here than you did at the cabin. You can pretty much do whatever you want on the property. There's four wheelers, bikes, you can hike some of the trails…get to know the outdoors a bit. Although with it being so hot, you probably won't want to go out too much until about October."

The Secret Life of Lies

Oklahoma City, huh. I guess it was random enough to keep me safe. Who would go looking for me in Oklahoma of all places? Also, I could only imagine how Bobby's thugs would stick out amongst the cowboys, so it was a pretty ingenious way to keep me safe. Remote, and anyone would recognize a stranger. Well done, Agent Wilcox, I thought as I smiled to myself.

"What?" he chuckled, "Why are you laughing?"

"Because I feel like I'm starting to understand all of this," I said, "I'm not sure if that's a good or a bad thing, really."

"Probably a good thing. This isn't going to be over any time soon, so you might as well make the best of it. It could be a couple of years before Bobby even goes to trial. You don't even go into the next phase of this until that happens."

"Which is witness protection."

"Yeeeeeeuuuuup," he sighed.

"That's a long time for Garcia to hate me," I said.

"Garcia doesn't hate you. I think quite the opposite. She's just at the point where she's deciding where she wants to go in the Bureau. It's not a job for everyone. Well, this part of the job, anyway. There are plenty of paper pushing jobs for those who want the 9-5 life. I think Garcia is doing what we all did at some point and deciding what she is and isn't willing to sacrifice for the job. If you want to be out here, you can't be there. Know what I mean?"

"Yes," I answered, "So is that what happened with you and your family?"

Wilcox made a face that resembled sucking on a lemon, then he sighed and relaxed. I immediately regretted saying that, because as I understood it, things weren't exactly copacetic with his daughter, Stephanie. We had briefly discussed his failed marriage and his grown daughter at the cabin while we were sort of getting to know each other, but I never asked these kinds of questions before. I was obviously terrible at this whole road trip thing.

"I-I-I'm sorry if that was out of line," I stammered, "I didn't mean for it to come out that way."

Wilcox checked his mirrors and looked at the dials on the dashboard, trying to look busy while thinking of something to say, I guess.

"No, I think it's a fair question to ask. Did my marriage fail and is my relationship with my daughter bad because I chose the job over them?"

I winced when he put it that way. I guess that's what I did say.

"No, I didn't choose the job over them. I told you, I'm not one of those Dudley DoRights that live, breathe, and die this job. I don't love my badge, and I'm not all that involved with the Bureau either. It was just something I was really good at that let me get out of my head and forget about the war. I loved Rita, my first wife. She made me feel normal, and maybe not so shell shocked, because when I came home, I was a damn mess. I'm talking liquid diet, pull me out of the gutter and wring me out. She loved me right out of that, and I wanted to show her my appreciation, so I gave her what I thought she wanted. I started here at the Bureau, worked local cases, bought a house, two cars, had Stephanie, a couple of dogs, the picket fence for the dogs, the whole shebang. And you know? I was really happy. I look back on those times and wish I could have done more with that than I did."

I kept my gaze out the window counting cacti as we drove, "Can I ask what happened? What went wrong with that life?"

"Oh I don't know, a lot of things," Wilcox sighed, "I probably should have seen a shrink, for starters. After a few years, I got bored and wanted to get more undercover and take on bigger cases. Rita wanted me home with her and the baby, and I started to feel suffocated with all of that. It wasn't that I didn't love them and want to be with them, but I just had this itch. I don't know how else to describe it, but this itch to keep moving. Like a shark, if I didn't keep swimming, I was going to die. So instead of being a man about things and just tell her like I'm telling you, I would come home from work every day, drink too many beers, say a bunch of mean shit to her, and made it her fault I hated my life. Well, she wasn't going to serve a life sentence of that, so she turned to the first guy who treated her right, and that was my buddy Lance. Lance was a good guy, he didn't mean to do me dirty, but of course I didn't see it that way."

I smiled, still looking out the window, "Let me guess. You rearranged his face when you found out he was being a little too friendly with your wife."

"Ha! I don't think Lance walked without a limp for a few years," Wilcox chuckled, "Actually I shouldn't laugh because I was a lunatic, and did enough damage that the Bureau almost shitcanned me. I was disciplined and finally sent to a shrink to get my head right, but by then it was too late. Rita and Lance were getting married, and she was moving Stephanie to Boston."

"I'm sorry," I said, "I really didn't mean to bring it up."

Wilcox shook his head, "Nah, don't be sorry. It was a long time ago and time takes care of pretty much everything," he reached into his back pocket for his wallet, and pulled out a picture, then handed it to me. It was a wedding picture of a beautiful auburn haired young woman in a white wedding dress, a handsome east coast upper crust looking guy in a tux, and Wilcox…in a tux. He actually looked good! He had that Vincent Vega look he had that first day he showed up on my doorstep, right down to that ridiculous earring, but he looked happy and handsome.

"That's Stephanie on her wedding day. She married a lawyer named Jack, and they're living the dream in Boston."

I laughed, "Look at you in the tux! You're adorable."

"First and last time I'll ever wear one of those," he smiled, "She said the same thing when she saw me. I'd do anything for that girl, even dress up like a penguin and sweat my ass off in the middle of July."

"You're a good dad, Dan," I said handing him the picture, "It probably didn't go the way any of you wanted, but she knew you loved her, and it looks like it all worked out."

"I suppose," he said, "You do remind me a lot of her. Or maybe you remind me a lot of myself."

"How's that?" I asked.

"You can't sit still either. If it was your idea, I don't think you would have a problem with staying in one place, but because we're telling you what to do, this is probably like prison for you. I also think you're mad at us for putting you here, when you should be mad at Bobby."

The Secret Life of Lies

"It's the gypsy heart," I said, "When I was little, my aunt always told me I had a gypsy heart because I had to be free and always wandered. And I am mad at Bobby, but the problem is I don't know how to be mad at Bobby yet. It's hard to explain, but I feel like I was married to a phantom or something. Like I believe in something that didn't exist. I can't see that person, I can't get closure, just like a mirage it vanished before my eyes. I can't rage at a figment of my imagination."

"I can see that, we'll have someone come in and help you out with that before the trial, and you'll come out of the shock when you're ready. Just don't wander in Oklahoma," he warned, "I hate rattlesnakes. I'm not looking for you if you take off, just so you know."

I laughed. I wish I would've met Wilcox under different circumstances. But I met him under these, and I firmly believe that everything happens for a reason. And I had Wilcox with me right now for a reason. I might have done something stupid and gone to see Bobby, but Wilcox was the reason I didn't go running back to San Diego and to my ultimate demise.

The rest of the ride was filled with joking, small talk, and music. Eventually we pulled off the highway and went through a series of city streets that turned into suburban avenues, and went into longer country roads. I bunched my nose up at the acrid smell of what had to be natural gas from the oil fields and the livestock. Wilcox laughed, "What you're smelling there princess is money!"

"God it's awful, worse than the cornstarch plants in Chicago," I said.

"You'll get used to it," he chuckled.

After what seemed like forever, we came upon a ranch with a sun beaten wooden gate. There was a sign nailed to it that said, "Treeland Ranch," and a gravel circular driveway enclosing a small pond with a water feature in front of the main house. Wilcox put the van in park and jumped out of the driver's seat to have a look at the pond. I got out and followed him.

"Damn!" he yelled with his hands on his hips looking down into the pond.

"What?" I asked.

"Damn frogs. I don't know how to keep the damn frogs in the pond. I just put a couple of frogs in here before I came to get you and now they've hopped away. What, are the fish scaring them or something?"

I had to laugh, because it was funny. Of all the things to worry about in a safe house, he was worried about keeping frogs in his koi pond.

"Oh you think this is funny? Do you know how many damn frogs I have tried to get to stay in this damn pond? I think I'm up to 20 now. I do everything right, I have the right PH level, the right food, adequate shelter, the works."

Well if that wasn't a metaphor for this current situation.

I looked down into the pond and noticed the pump churning away and making the water a bit rough, "I think you might have the water too unsteady in there. Maybe turn off the fountains for a while. I don't know anything about this, but don't frogs prefer swamps? Not much of a current in those waters, so maybe all of the activity is freaking them out."

"Ah, good point," Wilcox said, lighting a cigarette, "See Ava? I learned something," he exhaled a puff of smoke, "Why don't you get your stuff and settle in and I'll see about getting us something to eat."

CHAPTER 7

Johnston sat at his desk thinking. He had been watching Garcia and Wilcox like a hawk and had a few leads as to where Ava might be at this moment, but nothing definitive. He knew they had moved her from the Lake Tahoe safe house immediately after their encounter. Johnston had tailed her back after she had left the jail, but wasn't sure if the reason she had been moved was because she had told Wilcox what had happened, or they had figured it out. Part of him wanted to believe that it was coincidence because there was no change in where Bobby was housed, who had access to him, and no one said a word to Johnston about Ava or anything that had transpired. He only knew that when he was waiting for one of Bobby's guys to come up there and make the hit, Garcia tore out of there like a bat out of hell and onto the highway. Johnston followed her as long as he could, but a call from the office had him heading back to L.A. before he was missed. All he knew is they headed south and then west towards Reno.

The Secret Life of Lies

If any other agent were handling this case, he would've been able to crack it by now, but Wilcox made things difficult. He was old school, didn't even know how to turn on a computer, and wiped his ass with the 'Standard Operating Procedures' manual. The Bureau didn't care because he caught the bad guys and made them look good. He didn't work with anyone but Sorenson and Garcia, and they worked just like he did. Garcia was young, so she did log her reports and left somewhat of an electronic administrative trail, but not enough for Johnston to put the pieces together.

There was a close call with Wilcox not too long ago when Johnston was trying to snoop around his office for any clues and bug the phone. Bobby was breathing down his neck pretty hard for some good intel, and he had to come up with something to keep the money coming in and the gun away from his head so to speak.

"I'm not sure what you're looking for, Sonny Boy, but you're not going to find it in that desk drawer," Wilcox boomed from the doorway when he saw Johnston.

"Uh…you got a report cover?" he said trying to hide the fear in his voice.

"No. I haven't written a report since 1984," Wilcox answered, "And we have office supply closets for that shit. Why don't you try again and tell me what the fuck you're doing in my desk drawer in a locked office you aren't authorized to be in, in a division you don't work for, and we'll go from there, starting with your name."

"Agent Luke Johnston," he said coming around the desk with his hand outstretched to shake the older agent's hand, but Wilcox just stood there staring him down with an eyebrow raised.

Wilcox reached for the hand rolled cigarette behind his ear and with his eye still on Johnston, lit the end and inhaled deeply.

"You shouldn't smoke in here, sir," Johnston warned, bringing his still outstretched arm down to his side as Wilcox's eyes bored into his.

"Boy scout, are ya?" Wilcox laughed, walking past Johnston, having a seat in his worn leather desk chair, and propping his dusty boots on the desk, "If there's a problem with my smoking, I encourage you to file a report. I'll help you find the cover for that report, and I'll personally put it on the chief's desk for ya. You'll get a little gold star, and I'll get a nicotine patch to wear the one day a week I decide to grace this place with my presence."

"I meant no disrespect, I—" Johnston began.

"Johnston, is it?"

Johnston nodded.

"Well, Agent Johnston, here's what. I'm certain you weren't in here looking for a report cover because I'm pretty sure my reputation doesn't include 'copious note taker and report writer.' I'm also fairly certain you're looking for something from the case I'm working on because you might be entertaining someone who would have a vested financial interest in what might be going on with my witness."

Johnston opened his mouth to defend himself, but Wilcox held up a hand to stop him, "Save it. You seem to forget that I have been doing this much longer than you've been off your mother's teet. Consider yourself made. You're up to something, and you think it's worth it whatever it is," Wilcox took the final drag off his cigarette and put it out on the bottom of his boot, "I ain't no snitch, and I'm not afraid of punks, so I'm not going to go running to tattle on you. You'll show your ass eventually, you guys on the take always do. But let me give you a few words of advice," Wilcox stood and walked over to Johnston so they were almost nose to nose. Johnston could smell the fresh cigarette smoke on the older agent's breath and the sandalwood coming off his hair as the steel grey eyes met his in an intimidating stare.

"Agent Luke Johnston," Wilcox began in a low, yet fierce voice, "Go home tonight, open a beer, and go to the end of your living room. Watch your wife and your kids for a second as if they're in a movie. That movie always gets ugly. Always. Sure you're making the wife happy now with all that great pretend overtime pay and trips to Disney, the big house, the nice minivan with all the features, you're the pee wee football coach, the guy with the best neighborhood cookouts... but let me tell you something Agent Luke Johnston, that movie never ends well. You get in bed with dogs, you have some bad fleas when you wake up. The kind of fleas that will put bullets in the back of those kids' heads and rape your wife in front of you without batting an eye. So, if the money is worth it to you? Carry on. Now if you'll excuse me, I have to look like I'm doing paperwork for a while to keep the suits happy."

Without a word, Johnston headed for the office door, but Wilcox put a hand on his shoulder to stop him, the cold steel gray eyes piercing into his once again, "Oh and if you ever fuck with my witness again, you're going to wish you didn't."

Johnston felt his blood run cold as he made his way down the hallway back over to his office. So Wilcox did know something, but wasn't about to share who or what he knew, but Johnston believed he would make good on his threat.

That meeting stayed with him for a while, even prompting him to try to get out of the game with Bobby. Bobby of course refused and reminded him that promises were made, and promises had to be kept. Was Johnston alive and reaping the financial rewards of working for Bobby? So then Bobby was holding up his end of the bargain. Bobby Perez was smooth, but he was also relentless. He was putting the screws to Johnston to get rid of Ava sooner rather than later and as the trial came closer and closer, he knew that there had to be something done or Bobby would begin to lose his patience one way or another.

He sat there looking at the log in screen on the computer and knew he had only two more logins left before a security breach would happen and the failed log in attempt could be traced back to him. He had spent two days trying to watch Garcia and figure out how to access her files, and once he did crack some of the coded language they might be recorded in. So far kid's names, birthdays and anniversaries weren't the obvious passwords into her profile.

Based on what he had learned during his forensic IT rotation a couple of years ago, he decided to forgo the whole password cracking and try to hack in under his own account in order to backdoor his way in to her files through the main server.

After a few quick key strokes, he found himself in Garcia's profile and looking at countless files regarding the Perez case and Ava. He copied each of these onto a flash drive and quickly exited the hack before he could be detected, and covered his tracks. He then took the flash drive and loaded it onto his personal computer to see what he could make of all of it.

Most of the files were written in code. Some of it was standard and easy to decipher, but some of it was obviously in a language only Wilcox, Sorenson, and Garcia understood. There was one code word: TLX that kept coming up in some of the logs. Obviously it was a location, but where in the hell was TLX? It's not like there was a directory of every safe house in the country, because many of them were off the grid and only known to a few people involved in the investigation.

He sat at his desk staring at a map for what seemed like hours thinking about what TLX could possibly mean. It wasn't local, because Wilcox and Garcia were only in the office every 14 days or so, and they didn't fly in from where they were at. Wilcox was always covered in dust, which lead to somewhere in the Southwest, but that could be anywhere in a 1,000 mile radius. Hell, Nebraska was probably as dusty as Reno in the middle of August.

Johnston clicked on the folder icon again and looked at the reports from the date they left Lake Tahoe to now for any other clues when he came upon Sorenson using the code word, "Rig."

Rig…Johnston thought…oil…Texas? That was a bit obvious with the T and the X in the location code, so it really couldn't be that, and so close to Mexico would make it a security risk to have such a small detail of security around Ava. But he knew he was onto something with the oil reference.

On a hunch, he went back through some of the case file archives he had access to as a domestic intel agent, and with a bit of research was able to cross Texas off the list of possibilities. As he whittled down the field in the database, a clue jumped out at him.

Oklahoma.

Wilcox had worked a case back in the early 90's where he had to keep a witness safe after they had been found at a previous safe house location by the bad guys wanting to keep him quiet. There wasn't a specific location named, but Oklahoma seemed to fit the coded language they were all using. Especially 'Rig'.

Now he was onto something, Oklahoma wasn't that big and sussing out a safe house wouldn't be as tough now that he knew where to look.

CHAPTER 8

Wilcox returned to the hospital room the next morning to find Ava sitting up in bed looking better than she had since being shot. Her color was coming back, and while she was still frail, there was a spark back in her eyes. It made him smile.

"Well, look at you sitting up, good morning."

"Morning!," she chirped, "I was wondering when you would get here."

"Oh really?," Wilcox asked, "I was wondering if you'd ever be happy to see me again."

"I wouldn't say, 'happy,' but I wanted to talk about some more stuff."

"Yeah? Like what."

"Johnston. So you had an idea he was on the take from Bobby," Ava said.

Wilcox hesitated as he threw his leather jacket on the chair by the window and sipped his coffee, "I didn't know he was on the take then. Well, not like we know now. I thought maybe, maybe he was taking some cash from a low level thug of Bobby's in exchange for evidence or information about you. He was kid without all that much clearance, and his line of work in the bureau wouldn't really jive with what Bobby would be up to. How the whole thing lined up I'm still working on putting together. Had to move his wife and kids to a safe house today."

"Really?" Ava asked surprised.

"You're surprised by that?" Wilcox asked amused.

"I guess I didn't think there would be any more danger with everyone dead…" Ava trailed off.

"Oh, honey. Now we've got a power vacuum in two houses of organized crime. No one is safe. Agent Johnston's kids, Justin, Diana Knight…"

"Diana Knight!" Ava exclaimed.

"Yeah, what about her?"

"Don't trust Diana Knight," Ava warned.

"Why."

"I'll get to that, but before I do, leave this room and go call whoever you have to call to keep her wherever she's at. She's connected to both Johnston and Justin, and batshit insane. Make sure Justin is far away from her, and they're not communicating," Ava pressed.

"Oh, yeah…isn't she Justin's ex? I can see why you don't want them talking," Wilcox chuckled.

A wash of anger came over Ava's face, "Are you fucking kidding me, Dan? My sister is dead and you think I'm playing high school, don't steal my man bullshit, with a completely looney tunes bitch who helped orchestrate it? Fuck, no! I'm trying to prevent more people I love from dying. Let me tell you something about Diana Knight. She sees me as the single person responsible for ruining her life, so she's going to keep ruining mine until she succeeds. I'll give you every detail I have, but right now you have to go. Now."

"Okay," Wilcox said as he picked up his coat and marched out the door, coffee in hand.

* * *

My first encounter with Diana Knight was brief, and not very pleasant. She was a correspondent for one of the cable news networks, and she was thirsty for my story and dying of hunger to make a name for herself. She had contacts everywhere, and she wasn't afraid to call in favors when she needed them.

One of those contacts was Agent Luke Johnston, I would later find out years down the road. She and Luke had been childhood friends and had stayed in contact throughout the years as their careers intersected. She had good info, he would give her leads. It was a mutually beneficial relationship.

My run in with Ms. Knight happened after I had been in Oklahoma for almost a year. I wasn't happy by any means in my little prison at the Treeland Ranch, but I wasn't unhappy. I guess you could call it a bit of a 'bland content.' I managed to keep myself busy, occasionally Wilcox would let me go into town with him in disguise, and I had basically all of the creature comforts a human being could want, except I only ever saw two people, and I wasn't allowed to leave unless I was wearing a platinum blonde mullet wig Wilcox had found somewhere. Probably in the evidence room from a case involving a dead drag queen.

"I'm not wearing this," I glowered at him as he presented the blonde roadkill wig to me beaming.

"Aw c'mon! It's cute! You'd make a cute blonde!" He put on the wig, and it made him look like David Lee Roth as he pranced around the kitchen, I couldn't help but laugh.

"You couldn't find anything better than a platinum mullet?"

He pulled the wig off and tossed it to me with his grin still plastered to his face, "Disguise, kid. You seem to forget your face was all over the national news for almost a year. Can't have anyone recognize you. So if you want to go out, go put it on, and just wear something plain like a pair of jeans and a t-shirt with those cowboy boots. That way you'll blend in and no one will look at you for too long."

I looked at the limp nylon hair in my hands, "Yeah, if they don't wonder where the mental patient escaped from."

"Nah," Wilcox said, "In Oklahoma they'd just shoot you," he laughed while pulling his hair back into a ponytail and securing it with a rubber band, "See? I'm in disguise, too."

I laughed and headed up the stairs to my bedroom to get ready. I guess beggars can't be choosers when it comes to freedom.

***

We wound up at some kind of steakhouse slash honky-tonk where the floor was made of wood planks, and people threw peanut shells on the floor while waiting for

The Secret Life of Lies

their 24 oz porterhouse steak. There was a jukebox and a dance floor in the corner and a bar in the center of the place. Wilcox and I grabbed a booth in a dimly lit corner, nut shells crunching under our boots as we walked across the worn plank floor.

It was a Thursday night, and the place was moderately busy. Mostly people getting off work and having a happy hour drink and appetizer on their way home. A couple of families with children were scattered through the booth section, and Wilcox and I must have looked like any other father and daughter grabbing an early dinner.

I did notice a gorgeous blonde whooping it up with some cowboys over at the bar. She looked passingly familiar, like I might have seen her before, but not anyone I recalled knowing. Her hair was big, her laugh even bigger, and she looked like she was going to be saving a horse and riding one of those cowboys later. She must have seen me staring because she caught my eye and flashed a chiclet-white grin with lips coated in frosty lipgloss. I half smiled back and returned to my menu.

"So basically this place serves meat with a side of meat," I told Wilcox.

"And beer," he said.

The waitress came up and took our drink orders and Wilcox excused himself to go use the men's room while I sat there and picked at our giant deep fried onion appetizer. Wilcox loved these kinds of places, and I wondered how he must still be alive with the grease that must be coursing through his arteries.

I actually smelled Diana before I saw her. A cloud of Marc Jacobs perfume came my way, followed by the click-clack of sky high patent leather red high heels. She was like the poster child for 'tacky.'

"Hey there!" she drawled, "I've never seen you around here before! You new in town?"

"Not really," I said, "I've been here about a year."

"Oh, really? Where you from?"

"The midwest," I answered trying to keep it vague.

"Honey, me too! I'm from Chicago!" she squealed.

"I would've never guessed that by your accent," I said, "You sound like you're from here."

"Well, I could tell that you weren't from around here by yours," she paused while her eyes became snake like as she fixed them on me, "You might want to work on that if you want to fit in around here."

Before I could ask her what she meant by that, she broke her stare and looked up to see Wilcox returning from the men's room. She fixed her glossy beaming smile back on her face and turned her attention to him.

"Hey honey!" she exclaimed like they were old friends, "I was just asking your daughter here if she had a quarter for the jukebox, she doesn't, so do you have a one by chance, sugar?"

Wilcox flipped her a quarter without a word.

"Thank you, honey. Hey sweetie, I didn't get your name?"

I choked. Like literally choked. That was something we hadn't rehearsed.

"Stephanie," Wilcox chimed in, "She's Stephanie and I'm Rob."

Diana held out her hand and he shook it, "Well great to meet you, Stephanie and Rob, I hope to see you 'round here a lot more!" she chirped and then click clacked with her cloud of Marc Jacobs perfume following her, and sauntered back over to her cowboys.

I was done choking at this point, "The fuck?" I managed to get out.

"What?" Wilcox asked.

"I think we should go," I said, "I don't have a good feeling about this place. I'll tell you why on the way back."

"Ok," Wilcox said, taking out his billfold and leaving a couple of twenties on the table.

* * *

Johnston's phone rang at 7pm L.A. time. The call said, "Unknown" on the screen, but he knew it was Diana.

"Hello?"

"Hey, it's me," he could hear Diana's voice over what sounded like muffled country music.

"Where are you?"

"I'm at a place called the Steer Stockade just outside the city, calling from one of the few pay phones still in existence. I saw her."

"Ava?" Johnston asked.

"No, Hillary freaking Clinton. Yes, Ava. She and that Wilcox guy came in for dinner. She was wearing a blonde wig. They must be holed up close, then. This place is about 10 miles outside the city limits of OKC and there are really only three main drags that lead up to it. Should I follow them?"

"No," Johnston answered, "I'll figure out how to approach this next. How do you know it was her?"

"I talked to her," Diana answered flatly.

Upon hearing this, Johnston put his palm to his face, "Christ, Diana, why the FUCK would you do that? I told you not to approach them. Now you probably blew our cover and Wilcox is going to move her tonight."

"Why?" Diana began to argue, "Because some bar fly came up and asked for a quarter for the jukebox?"

"I have a hard time believing that's all you said," Johnston replied.

"Hey, I want this scoop," Diana said, "I'm sitting here in bumblefuck Oklahoma looking like some kind of Dolly Parton reject because I want this story on her. You promised me that exclusive when I found her, and now I've found her, so you have to pay up, pal."

Johnston sighed, "Yes, I will get you that exclusive, but you can't just march up to a safe house and knock on the door. You don't know what kind of security detail is on that place, and the second they interrogate you, it leads back to me."

"Oh you think I'm that weak? That I'd give you up?" Diana balked.

"No, but I don't think you've been interrogated very much, either. Now, you hang tight and I will get you your exclusive by the end of the weekend. Do not breathe a word of this to anyone, because if there's a chance you didn't get peeped by Wilcox, we have to keep this under wraps. So go have another beer and learn some more line dances. I'll call you in the morning."

"But—"

Johnston hung up the phone before Diana could say anything else and opened his laptop to access the satellite maps of Oklahoma. After locating the coordinates to the Steer Stockade, he began to examine the lay of the land

and where the safe house might be located. He combed the three roads leading in to the outer limits of the city, and he hit pay dirt on the smallest of them that headed just north. After about five miles he saw a ridge and a forest just behind a gully. Behind that forest was a clearing and a ranch.

Pay dirt.

* * *

"I think you're just being paranoid," Wilcox said as he tipped back the bottle to get the last of his beer, as we sat on the back deck with a fire going.

"Are you serious?" I challenged, "Really? I'm in a safe house because the FBI is paranoid. I'm telling you, something was up with that one."

He shrugged, "Maybe. I think it was more a case of someone thinking you were the chick that stole her man and she thought she would tell you what's up with the benefit of liquid courage," he tossed his bottle into the fire pit, "No one would even think you were here. This is the remote of the remote, and so classified only my team knows. I can't imagine anyone thinking you were here of all places. But I'm glad to hear you want to be cautious. If it makes you feel better, we'll call in an extra security detail to watch the place just in case. You okay with that?"

I agreed with him, but I was still uneasy about it. My gut had failed me over and over again, but now it was letting me know this wasn't okay. Although I trusted Wilcox, I couldn't shake the feeling that the trashy blonde in the bar was specifically talking to me. It was haunting.

* * *

Wilcox came back into the hospital room to find Ava scribbling furiously into a notebook on her lap. She didn't even look up when she heard the door close. He stood there watching her for a minute waiting for her to break her concentration.

"Ok, I made the call. What are you working on there?" he asked.

Ava let out a sigh and sat back in the bed and closed her eyes, "It really is my fault, you know."

"I wouldn't go that far. You made some truly horrible decisions, but you're human. Humans are fallible. It's the whole nature of the beast thing, you know?"

Ava rolled her eyes, "No. That's not what I mean. I mean, I don't even know, like, if I had told you about what happened at the ranch a few days after we ran into Diana at the bar -"

Wilcox cut her off, "But you did tell me about Diana. I just thought you were being paranoid. That was my bad. And what happened at the ranch? There was security all over the place. Unless of course—"

"Johnston decided he wanted to work security that day," Ava finished.

Wilcox started to pace slowly in front of the bed, "But that would be impossible because I was sort of on to him for other reasons and made sure to tell both Garcia and Sorenson that if Johnston was sniffing around the case anymore to tell me, and I'd have that punk sent back to the U.S. Marshalls picking up old hookers on 15 year old county warrants. Besides he was in IT, and there would be no way a computer guy would get approved to do classified tactical work or get anywhere near a witness." He stopped pacing for a minute and stared out the window to collect his thoughts while Ava sat watching him quietly.

"But you think if you would've told me he showed up at the ranch, things would be different, which maybe. I don't know. Would you still have gone to Chicago?"

"At this point? I don't know. My sister is dead. If I didn't get off at that exit all those years ago, she may still be alive. I guess nothing makes sense when you look back on it. But maybe if I had told you about Johnston's cameo at the ranch, the second half of the story wouldn't have happened."

Wilcox shook his head and quit looking out the window and return his attention to Ava, "I suppose I should tell you that we're holding Diana for questioning now."

Ava raised an eyebrow, "Connected the dots did ya?"

"Yep," he sighed, "Another simple thing that slipped right on by. I think the lesson here is that things are ridiculously simple, but we expect them to be complicated. I don't know. As I see what happened, I wonder if I was too old for the job. Some of this shit makes me look downright senile. I was in over my head, and I also feel like this is on me. Had I known about your family, Maria, put the screws to Johnston when I had the chance, I don't know, maybe none of us would be here right now. It's a bitch."

"That it is," Ava smiled wanly.

"Well, let's keep going so we can make the bad decisions right. Tell me what happened that day at the ranch when Johnston showed up, and most of all, why didn't you tell me?"

"Honestly," Ava began, "I didn't tell you because I didn't want to leave again. Even though I was still isolated and still not living a normal life, I felt safe. I felt like I had more normal days, and I felt like I could think things through, like I was finally able to face and work through what happened. I didn't have to run and look over my shoulder because I finally allowed myself to trust you and trust you were doing right by me. I just didn't want to have another upheaval in my life. I didn't have another one in me."

Wilcox took a seat in his normal spot in the corner, "Yeah. I don't know where I would've taken you at that point if you had told me. You would've had to go to an Embassy or something. Especially with Johnston all over us like flies on shit," he rubbed his temples with his fingers, obvious exhaustion showing on his aging face, "Tell me about that day, what went down."

"I should've killed that spider, that's what."

CHAPTER 9

I don't kill spiders. I relocate them. I guess it comes with having overly superstitious old world relatives. I was actually more afraid of the bad luck killing a spider would bring me more than I was afraid of the actual spider. Then of course I would start thinking about the spider and its little spider family, the little spider babies, and I just simply couldn't kill another living creature. But this one should have died.

The spiders in Oklahoma were gigantic. These weren't itty bitty attic spiders, or even the big fuzzy tree spiders that always look like Halloween, these were spiders practically big enough to carry away a baby. When you saw them you instinctively yelped, and froze for a second.

That morning as I was rounding into the kitchen from my bedroom for a cup of coffee, I saw one of these giant spiders hanging out on the white wall in the hallway. I jumped, squeaked a little, and continued into the kitchen for a cup to put the spider into and relocate it outside. Within a few minutes I was walking out the back sliding door into the backyard. I walked down the gravel path into the tree line behind the house and bent over to let the bug free.

That's where I ran into Agent Johnston.

He was dressed in head to toe camo and with the quickness of a cat, pounced on me and with his hand on my sternum, pushed me into the nearest tree, knocking the wind out of me so I couldn't scream, and gaining the upper hand while I lay there on the ground gasping for any breath to enter my lungs. I struggled to breathe, and get my bearings. I knew I would be in for a fight.

Soon I had air again, and my brain started to work. Wilcox had increased security, so all I had to do was get to the house and be seen. I couldn't just make a run for it the way I came, because he could overtake me in a short sprint, no doubt. Now was the time to put all of the running I had been doing to kill time to the test. I could outrun him over a couple of miles through the hilly tree line back to the house. I knew the terrain, the lay of the land, and I could run up on the east side of the ranch and be seen by one of the guards. It was a great plan, except for one thing…

I wasn't wearing shoes.

Guess I would be making my debut as a barefoot trail runner.

As I lay there catching my breath, I saw Johnston pull zip ties from his cargo pocket, and he squatted down to get close to my face, "Gotcha" he whispered, his blue eyes locking on mine. Without even thinking, I picked up my head from the ground and with all the force I could manage I rammed my forehead into his lower jaw, which caused me to see stars, but I heard a crunch that would buy me a few seconds, and I took off running.

The Secret Life of Lies

With the adrenaline coursing through my veins, both fight and flight kicking in, I ran as fast as I could through the woods up the hill and out towards the east clearing by the ranch. I didn't bother to look behind me to see if Johnston was on my tail, because I didn't want to lose precious speed, and pumped my arms and legs like I had never done in my life before that moment. Soon I saw the clearing and rounded the corner around some old stables, and felt the sharp pebbles under the soles of my feet as the dirt of the small forest turned into the sand of the corral.

As I came past the stable I saw the guy that was usually at that post, and gave a big wave and 'Hey!' to make sure he saw me, and to let Johnston know he saw me. There was nothing stopping Johnston from shooting me in the back, but at least he'd thing twice about it now knowing that someone else could shoot back.

The guard waved back at me with a half nod, probably assuming I was out for one of my normal runs because I was in sweats, and he probably couldn't tell I was barefoot, and I cleared the stables and made my way to the lawn that led back to the yard and the back deck into the kitchen.

Johnston wouldn't be following me this far. I had run to safety. For now, anyway.

I ran into the house, locked every door, and ran to the master bathroom, slamming and locking the door behind me. I looked down at my bloodied, dirty feet, and opened the bathroom door to see dirty, bloody footprints leading from the back sliding door to the bathroom. Quickly, I ran out to the kitchen and grabbed a rag and some cleaning spray and hastily wiped up the evidence of my run for my life through the woods. I returned to the bathroom and locked the door behind me. Now I looked at my reflection in the mirror, and saw a goose egg forming on my forehead where I had head butted Johnston. Upon seeing myself, tears welled in my eyes and I ran to the toilet to vomit.

Then I went to the shower and turned the water to as hot as I could possibly stand and climbed in, letting the sobs overtake me and stood there heaving and shaking until the hot water ran out. When the water ran cold, I shut off the faucet, wrapped myself in a towel, and fell into my bed nude, where I stayed most of the day. I couldn't think about anything. I couldn't feel anything. I just sank into a dark abyss.

* * *

The light knocking on my bedroom door woke me from my sleep. I must have been out for a long time because the sun was setting and the light coming through my window had that pinkish hue of late afternoon. I rose out of bed and I was taken aback by the soreness of my muscles. The fresh cuts on my feet burned and my head still throbbed.

Then my stomach did a flip flop and my heart began to race. What the hell was I going to tell Wilcox?

I threw on my robe, hobbled over to the door, and opened it a crack. Wilcox was standing in the hallway, wearing his dusty leathers from his ride.

"Hey, you ever get up today? Feeling okay?" He asked.

"Um…" I hesitated and took a deep breath, opening the door to let Wilcox in my room, while I walked back to my bed to sit down, because standing that long had made me dizzy, "Yeah, I got up and saw a spider, so I trapped it in a cup and carried it outside to the woods to let it free…and…"

Wilcox noticed the bump on my head, "The fuck happened?"

Tell the truth, Ava. Tell the truth, Ava. Just tell him.

"Um…I saw a coyote, or I think I saw a coyote and I took off up the hill. I slipped and smacked my head on a rock, and my feet were cut up pretty badly," I showed him my bloody feet.

"Shit," he whistled, "A coyote? Pretty strange they'd be out in the morning."

Crap. He knows I'm lying to him. Why do I keep lying to this guy?

"Let me see that lump on your head," he said walking over towards my bed. He tilted my chin back gently with his fingers to see my forehead better in the light, "Follow my finger," he said holding up his index finger and moving it side to side while my eyes tracked it.

"Well, you conked your head really hard, but I don't think you did any permanent damage. One of the good things about being as hard headed as you are," he chuckled, "Come on downstairs and and let's get some bacitracin on those feet before you get gangrene and I have to saw them off in the tool shed, Old West style," he smiled at me, patted me on the shoulder, and headed out of my room back down the hallway, the heels of his boots making muffled clacks on the floor.

I hated myself for lying to him. He's probably the only person in this world who really cares about me at this point, and here I am lying to him for no real reason besides being afraid of the truth. If I tell him about

Johnston, then he'll know I've lied to him about other things, too. I didn't want to disappoint him. Maybe I should ask him when I'm going to see that shrink. Obviously my mind wasn't right anymore.

* * *

"Turns out you broke his jaw," Wilcox said scratching his temple and looking out the window, "That hard noggin of yours hit him like a wrecking ball."

Ava smiled wanly, "Really? How do you know that?"

"Well, when you go to sleep after our little talks, I head out and try to put some pieces together for myself. I looked into where Johnston was those days and he wasn't in San Diego or L.A. He had taken five days off for personal time, and then he had to take another three weeks off because he had broken his jaw in a freak hunting accident. You would think the FBI would wonder what the fuck an agent would be hunting in late summer, as really nothing in North America is in season, except maybe protected witnesses…" he trailed off, "So for someone who won't even squish a spider, you will head butt a man so hard his jaw breaks. Now there's a dichotomy."

Ava looked down at her hands, Wilcox was still looking out the window, "I'm sorry I lied to you, I'm so sorry," tears began streaming down Ava's face, "I don't know what was wrong with me. You were the only person who really cared about me, well besides Maria, but I couldn't see or talk to her then, and I just kept lying and putting us in danger. I'm so sorry," Ava was now sobbing, "So, very, very, sorry."

The Secret Life of Lies

Wilcox turned his gaze from the window and looked at Ava, tiny, pale and fragile, sobbing her heart out in that hospital bed and his heart broke. Tears welled up in his own eyes as he saw this broken woman sobbing.

"Ava," he began his voice breaking, "I should have gotten you more help. You were so good at acting like you were handling everything okay, I just figured you dealt with it in your own way, and you were going to be okay on your own. You struck me as the type that saved her tears for her pillow, and were going to tough your way out. I'm sorry, too."

Wilcox stood up and walked over to Ava's bed, sitting next to her and enveloped her in his arms. Ava could smell the sandalwood and patchouli, and began to cry even harder. Wilcox sat there and held her silently with tears rolling down his cheeks until she fell asleep.

The last time he hugged her, she broke his heart. This time would be different.

* * *

My wounds eventually healed, and there weren't any more incidents at the ranch for the rest of the time I was there until Bobby's trial. Wilcox and Garcia took good care of me, and my days went by as fast as they possibly could. Closer to the trial they became very busy with prosecutors rehearsing my testimony and preparing me for extensive cross examination, how I would handle any media, and the next phase of my life.

It was so hard to even think about the next phase of my life, because the last two years had been such a series of temporary arrangements, I wasn't even sure what a permanent life would feel like. I avoided the conversation as much as possible, because the idea of having a permanent life and then losing it for a third time would be almost too much to bear, so I chose not to bear it.

I adopted a very 'first things first' policy for my life. First thing I had to do was survive Oklahoma, then the trial.

CHAPTER 10

Over the next couple of years, the media let up on Ava, and Bobby's case was replaced by dozens of other things going on in the world that captured the incredibly short attention span of people today. In a way, Maria was grateful for that because it meant that Ava would be able to have somewhat of a quiet life once this was over, wherever and whenever that may be.

Maybe she would even get to see her again.

She had tried to put feelers out there to see where Ava might be, or if there might be a way to get in touch with her, but each time she ran into a dead end. Wherever Ava was, she was hidden well. It was another thing that gave Maria some peace of mind, because she knew the kind of goons drug cartel guys had, and guys like Bobby would stop at nothing to silence people.

While the media let the case fall by the wayside, the internet and secondary cable networks never let it go. There were a couple of websites devoted to people obsessed with the case who sat in chat forums all day picking apart each and every aspect of the case. Maria referred to them as the, 'Cat Ladies Detective Agency,' because these people had to be shut ins based on the sheer number of hours they spent researching things online. And half the time, they weren't even right! The cat ladies had Ava growing up in another suburb, changing her name at 19, and taking a train to Los Angeles to become an actress after she had dropped out of junior college after one failed semester. It was hysterical to Maria how this completely false narrative had been written, and this group of people completely bought it. If that wasn't a commentary on the current state of the world, Maria was glad her internet presence was virtually nothing.

She did hang around those forums to get some of the legal information these nutters were obtaining through FOIA requests. Maria poured through the released documents to see what the government had on Bobby. It also in a roundabout way made Maria feel closer to Ava knowing what was happening in her world.

The cable station LegalTV would be broadcasting the trial live as it happened. Maria looked up at the calendar, opening arguments were marked in red pen for tomorrow at 11a.m. Chicago time. Mostly she was eager to see Ava when she was called to testify. It would be the first time she had seen or heard her in years.

In those years since Bobby had been caught, Maria's life hadn't changed all that much. She had taken over some of the business from Uncle Angelo after he had suffered a minor stroke. She ran certain parts of the various businesses in the 'import/export' business while the rest of the family busied themselves with spending his money. Life was going to be a huge mess when Uncle

Angelo died, so she should at least be the one to know the business and keep everyone in Cadillacs.

When the trial started, it seemed like a pretty cut and dried case. The government had a mountain of evidence against Bobby that was staggering. Ava didn't even need to testify, really, it would just be a formality.

Bobby's defense?

You got the wrong guy, copper.

Maria had to roll her eyes at that one. Good luck with that, buddy.

After a couple of days of expert witnesses discussing boring forensic details of the case, the prosecution called Ava to the witness stand. Before they did, they had filed a motion to not have her face televised during her testimony to keep her identity secret, and of course, Bobby's defense team balked at this, because how was he supposed to have her killed if people forgot what she looked like?

It made Maria seethe with anger that she had allowed herself to be duped by such a slimeball.

The prosecution won their argument, and Ava would not be shown on the broadcast while she testified. The cameras were instructed to show only the seal of the United States of America during Ava's testimony or the lawyers questioning her. If they showed Ava's face, a mistrial would be declared with stiff penalties for whatever network made the error.

Maria's stomach lurched when she heard the clerk call, "Ava Giancola."

* * *

The female prosecutor on the case, Sylvia Normandy, smiled at me as I took my seat in the witness box. The courtroom was packed with media, and Bobby sat at the defense table in a designer suit, polished shoes, and groomed to perfection. I didn't recognize that Bobby, because the Bobby I knew was usually casually dressed with a day of scruff on his face and tousled hair. Jail had aged him quite a bit, and he sat there staring at me with a hard set in his jaw. If looks could kill, I would be dead ten times over already. My knees were shaking as I sat there in the leather office chair, and I was glad for the wood partition in front of me so no one could see how nervous I was.

Sylvia and I had practiced for this moment over countless hours at the ranch. We went over the questions she would ask, some of the horrible things the defense might ask and accuse of me, and how she would redirect those questions. I was coached on how to breathe, compose myself, address the jury, and keep my head if Bobby's lawyers went all in on me. I was as prepared as I possibly could be, but it was still utterly terrifying.

"Please state your name for the record," Sylvia said.

"Ava Giancola," I answered.

"And how do you know the defendant?" She asked pointing to Bobby.

"He's my husband," I answered.

"You're married to Roberto Raul Perez?" She asked with mock horror.

"No ma'am," I answered, "I married Robert Joseph Giancola in San Diego eight years ago. That's who I married. I was not aware Roberto Raul Perez even existed."

The Secret Life of Lies

There was murmuring in the courtroom when I said that, but Sylvia ignored it and went on with her questioning. Basic stuff, really, and supported my answers with the documents Wilcox had shown me about the real Bobby Giancola and the identity the Perez family had stolen in order to have an American son.

I wound up being questioned by Sylvia for two full days. At the end of each day, I was whisked in an armored car from underneath the federal building and taken to the Hyatt Regency in downtown Los Angeles, through the underground loading dock reserved for people like the President of the United States and Beyonce. It was very strange. I felt like I was starring a movie about someone else's life.

I was also strange to recount every detail in front of an entire room of people and cameras. Even though my face was never shown, my testimony was broadcasted, and I had to recount every single moment of those days after Wilcox showed up on my doorstep. Everything from the discovery in his office, the night he beat me up, the raid, Wilcox carrying me out after the shoot out, all of it.

I had been afraid that reliving the whole saga would just pick the scab of those wounds back open and I would totally fall apart over the life and love I had lost, but in reality it served as closure for all of it. As I laid out the narrative of my discovery of who Bobby really was, I let him go. I realized that I never really knew who Bobby was in the first place, so to mourn something that didn't exist was a waste of energy. These were my last moments as Ava Giancola, because when I left this courtroom for the last time, I would have a new identity.

So I testified, and buried Ava at the same time.

When Sylvia was done, the judge let Bobby's lawyer, a high profile defense attorney I had seen before on TV, know I was his witness. I took a deep breath and started to prepare myself for the worst. I was trying so hard to quiet my internal screaming I barely heard the man say, "No questions for this witness, your honor."

Again the courtroom was buzzing and my head snapped up to attention. What? No questions for me? Bizarre. I made the mistake of looking at Bobby at that moment and he just sat there smiling at me.

That's it. It's over for me. I don't ever have to see him again. I have my life back.

Rest in peace, Ava Giancola.

* * *

"We the jury find the defendant Roberto Raul Perez, guilty…" A woman's voice on the television said as Maria filled a drink order and worked on other business at her desk. She reached over for the remote sitting on a stack of papers and switched it off. That was the eleventh guilty verdict, and she was satisfied that Bobby wouldn't be seeing the light of day outside of barbed wire for a few lifetimes.

"Now you're free," she said softly to herself as a wave of sadness washed over her while looking a framed picture of Ava from her days at the Joffrey on her desk. It almost felt like a death to have the trial over, because there would be no more news or connection to Ava's life for at least a long time. Maria knew a little about witness protection, and she knew you couldn't reach out to family members for at least 10 years. Obviously, and rather smartly, Maria noted, Ava didn't let on to having any family to speak of, because in the years leading up to the trial, none of the men in black ever showed up on her doorstep to let her know the protocol.

She only hoped that the years would go by quickly enough that it wouldn't feel like forever before she saw Ava again.

CHAPTER 11

After my testimony at the trial, I went back to the ranch with Wilcox, Sorenson and Garcia to prep for the last leg of this journey, and that was good old witness protection. They had a fancy less made-for-TV-drama word for it in the FBI, but basically it was what you know as the witness protection program.

I'll spare you the endless days of boring protocol that I had to go through, but the gist of it was I was no longer Ava Giancola. As soon as we got in the car for the ride back from California, the three of them started calling me 'Ms. Clark.'

It was so weird. No first name yet, mostly because I don't think they even had one, just 'Ms. Clark.'

Wilcox just addressed me as, "Hey," or "You," because I think it was even weirder for him.

Once we made it to the ranch, I was given the name Rebecca. I rolled my eyes so hard they almost fell out of my head.

"Becky Clark? Are serious? You guys are punking me, right? You can't seriously have picked that for me," I laughed.

"I said 'Rebecca,'" Sorenson deadpanned.

"What?" Wilcox smiled, "Becky Clark is a cute name! What's wrong with it? You could be a Becky—"

Garcia choked down a snort-laugh.

"Nevermind," I sighed.

Wilcox smiled, "Listen, I know you're used to your super fancy name, but you have to have a common name so you don't stick out like a sore thumb, okay? People are going to be tracking you down. If you get a job, you're going to be Googled, and so on. The idea here is blending. I'm sorry you don't get to be the ballerina with a cool name anymore, but at least you won't be dead."

That got a pointed look from Garcia, and I just decided to shut my mouth at that point. No sense in arguing. Garcia handed me a sheet of paper and told me to start practicing my signature so they could get the appropriate documents together. I quietly complied.

Over the next couple of weeks, I became Rebecca. I was given a completely new biography, education, and Ava was pretty much wiped away. I even got a makeover to change the way I looked so I wouldn't be as easily recognized. My hair was cut into a long bob with blonde highlights, and even my accent was worked on so I wouldn't be such a dead giveaway like I was to Diana in the bar.

Based on my aptitude tests, because they had to determine my skills for working beyond being a dancer, and it turns out I'd make a really great secretary, so my new career was that of administrative assistant. I had transcripts telling the world I had a Liberal Arts degree from a small all women's college in Oregon, and I could type 70 words per minute accurately.

Becky Clark was boring as shit.

But I like boring, right? So I'm not sure why this bugged me so much. I think it irked me because I still felt like I was being punished for other people's crimes. Bobby had been convicted on all counts and would be spending the rest of his life behind prison walls, but he still got to be him. I wasn't even allowed to speak the same way anymore.

* * *

At the end of those two weeks of learning my new life: what to do, what not to do, how to answer, "You look like Ava Giancola," questions, I finally received my walking papers so to speak. Wilcox brought the banker's box out to the living room after dinner and set it on the coffee table.

"Well, the time has come," he said lifting the lid off the box, "Rebecca Clark, I introduce you to your new life!"

I know he meant well, but it really just put a pit of despair in the middle of my gut to see another chapter of my life, reduced to a box. It must've been written all over my face, because Wilcox jumped into action and tried to lighten the mood.

"C'mere, let me show you your house!" he exclaimed as he pulled out a binder and sat next to me on the couch. Inside were pictures of a cute little brick ranch house on a well manicured middle class suburban street. There were rose bushes in the front walkway, and a sitting area on the covered porch. It was cute, actually. I smiled a little when I saw it.

"See!" Wilcox said, "It's not so bad. I think you could do a lot with the place. Maybe get a dog or something, I don't know. It's got a decent fenced in backyard," he said flipping to the page to show me, "And you've got tons of room inside. All new appliances, the whole shebang."

"Where is it?" I asked.

"Just outside Stanford," he said quickly as if it were nothing.

"Like, Connecticut?" I asked.

"Yes," he answered.

Well, on the bright side, I hadn't ever been there, so it would be ok. I hadn't seen snow in years. This might actually not be the worst thing after all.

Wilcox and I spent the next few hours going through the box and talking about my new life in Connecticut. My car would be delivered tomorrow, and I would be on my way, just an administrative assistant heading out east after a bad breakup. I would have enough money and credit to get me through very comfortably for about six months, and I would need to check in with the witness protection liaison within five days of arriving to make sure I was okay and continue to check in periodically and I would also periodically be monitored.

So in other words, "You're never too far from the family," I said.

"Pretty much."

I put down the folder with my new financial information in it, "So what are you going to do after I drive off tomorrow?"

"Hop on my bike, ride off into the sunset, and retire from this bitch. My sentence is up," Wilcox said beaming.

I laughed, "I was that bad, huh?"

"Nah, kid, *life* was that bad. You were actually kind of a bright spot in the whole thing," he said.

My face flushed, "Awww, Dan!" I said in mock embarrassment, "That's the nicest thing you've ever said to me!"

Then an awkward silence fell between us.

"I'm never going to see you again, am I?" I asked.

"No kid. You probably won't. That's protocol. Whether I'm retired or not. People watch me too, ya know, and if I were ever in Stanford looking for trouble, I would bring anyone looking for you through me right to your doorstep."

I felt the tears start to fill my eyes, and I willed them not to roll down my cheeks, but I couldn't stop them. They came freely and Wilcox scooted over on the couch to hug me.

"It's okay, kid. You're just scared right now, and it's going to be okay. Pretty soon, and you'll see, this will be a memory. In a few years, I'll just be that rough old guy who got you through a bad time, and you'll smile a little, then one of your kids will break something and you'll have to go deal with that. This feeling isn't forever," he released me from his embrace and tilted my chin up, wiping my tears with his weathered thumb, "You're a good girl, Ava. A really good girl, and you will have the wonderful life you deserve. I know it."

He let me go and started to pack the box containing my new life, "You need to get some sleep. You have a very long drive ahead of you, and a long few days ahead." He was trying to disguise the sadness in his voice, but I could hear it.

* * *

Wilcox knocked on my bedroom door at 5:45 in the morning, and I wasn't sure I had slept more than 30 minutes the night before. I got up and ready for the day, and met him in the kitchen, where he was making me the now customary 'egg slop' as he called it, and my coffee was waiting for me as it always was on the breakfast bar.

"Aww! My farewell egg slop! Gee, Wilcox, you shouldn't have!"

"You like it. I know you do."

"What's not to like about a bowl of runny eggs, cheese and ham?" I smiled.

We ate breakfast together like it was any other morning with the news on the television in the background.

"Looks like you're going to have good weather today," Wilcox tried to say brightly.

I was about to answer him when a horn honked outside.

"Your car is here," Wilcox said, draining his cup and heading for the front door.

I followed him out, sort of excited about seeing my new car.

It was a Ford Taurus. Of course it was. Not that there's anything wrong with that, but you would think with a fleet of no less than 10,000 of these cars, the FBI would have a bit more imagination.

"I should have known it'd be a damn Taurus," I said with mock disdain.

"Sorry, princess. The federal government doesn't have a contract with Land Rover."

So here I was, Becky Clark, a small town girl heading east in my Ford Taurus to my quaint little life in Connecticut. I guess it could be worse.

After Wilcox talked to the agents who brought the car, and spec'ed it all out, we began to load it up with my banker's box, and the same bag of stuff I had been carrying around with me for the last couple of years. My house was already furnished, and I had been given money to purchase a more permanent wardrobe and any other incidentals I needed."

"Now you're going to stop for the night in Missouri," Wilcox instructed handing me an envelope, "Here's the hotel info. You're already checked in, all of your amenities are paid for, and after that, you'll stop in Schererville, Indiana, some town in Penn I've never heard of, and then you should be home. All your stuff is laid out for you there, and the car has GPS in it to get you there. Just punch in each hotel's address. You need me to show you how?" He asked.

I really didn't need him to show me, but I got the sense he wanted to be useful, so I pretended to need his help plugging in the first stop. When he was done with that, he scribbled a phone number on a piece of paper and handed it to me.

"When you get to Missouri, you call this number, let it ring twice, and hang up," he instructed, "And if you run into trouble along the way, you go to a pay phone at a truck stop, because they still have those there, preferably one of those tables with phones so you can be seen on camera, and you stay there and keep calling until I answer, okay?"

I smiled, "Is this protocol, sir?"

"I ain't about to start protocol on my last day," he said shutting the driver's side door then leaning in the window, "Be careful. It's going to be okay, BeckyAva."

I had to laugh at that, "Thank you for saving me. You have been so good to me through all of this."

"You've been good for me too, kid. I suppose I should tell you before you go that Stephanie called me an informed me this morning that I am going to be a grandpa again."

"Oh! That's so great! I'm glad you guys are talking more. And now you'll have more time to see each other. I'm really happy for you, Dan."

He smiled, sighed, and stood up, "Ok, time to fly little birdie. You still remember how to drive?"

"Hope so," I said putting the car into gear.

He nodded and walked away patting the trunk of the car twice as my cue to take off. I stared crying again and smiled through my tears as I watched him get smaller and smaller in my rearview mirror.

The next leg of my journey had officially begun.

CHAPTER 12

Wilcox leaned back in his chair and Ava heard it creak against his weight. He looked so worn and tired, and there was a sadness to him she hadn't noticed until this point. He let out a sigh and returned to his sitting position and rested his chin on hands propped up by elbows on knees.

"The psych team said you were ready, so I let you go," he said quietly, "I had a nagging feeling about you that I couldn't quite describe, but I just chalked it up to the fact that I had gotten close to you, and really didn't want you to go. It was nice feeling like a father figure again, and I thought maybe I was the one who needed a shrink."

"I was okay when I left," Ava replied.

"You made it not even a thousand miles before you weren't okay. You kept secrets, ran from the safe house before, so no…you were not okay, Ava. You were just a good liar," he said matter of factly.

Ava bristled at being called a liar so starkly, "So that's it? You just think I'm a run of the mill ol' liar then?"

"I didn't say that," he answered.

The Secret Life of Lies

"You did in not so many words," Ava fired back, "Even after hearing everything, you still go right back to that old chestnut. I'm just a secretive liar who lies all the lies because it's fun for me or something. Not at all out of fear of the unknown, grief for the life I lost, grief for the husband I believe I had, being sequestered from society for years, a fucking punk agent after me because there's a price on my head, all of those things that if I cried about them, or acted like they crippled my mind on a daily basis would only serve to lengthen my prison sentence with the FBI even though I was the victim in all of this? You have got to be kidding me, Dan. Really."

Wilcox lifted his head off his hands and gave Ava a puzzled look, "So you then come at me all guns blazing over the word, 'liar'. I didn't give that word any context, you did. You think I don't know that we don't lie to ourselves on some level in order to survive awful things? How many times I had to do something dirty for the greater good and I had to tell myself a sweet ass lie to make it more palatable? You were a good liar. I was a good liar, too. I told myself the lie that you were okay. Turns out, I wanted you to be solid and sane because I do carry a bit of guilt around that I essentially did my job so well it fucking destroyed your life, and then I didn't do my job so well and it destroyed your sister's and many others. So shut up, Ava. We both got it fucked. The only difference is, I actually knew better. I should have had you escorted. I could have gone the distance to make sure you made it. But you know what Ava? You want to know the truth? I was sad. I didn't want to work anymore. I wanted to get on a boat, park it on some sand, and forget this whole life of bullshit. I spent my whole career uprooting families when you think about it. That's the truth. The lie is truth, justice and the American way. We're all liars, Ava. You just happen to be good at it for better or worse."

* * *

I mostly lived in my head while I drove through the endless plains heading north east. I thought about all of those years past and tried to get excited about my future. Mostly I was wondering how I would get back to a life without someone. For the first time since I left the Joffery, I was totally on my own.

I also thought about leaving my life behind. Being sequestered for so long, I was very used to not having a connection to very many people and I had almost hardened myself to the idea that I had lost anything, really. Looking back, it had to be self preservation, because I think feeling any more than I had would have landed me a padded cell with a straight jacket.

Southern Missouri floated by and I stayed the night in the first hotel. It was nice to be alone and do what I wanted to do, but I was hollow in my loneliness. I kept expecting Wilcox to come through the door holding a bag of fried food in one hand and a six pack of beer tucked under the other arm, with that silly grin on his face, getting ready to tell me some great adventure or conversation he had on his run. But it never happened. It was like I was sitting there waiting for his ghost to visit. Another person that had died to me while still remaining alive.

As I sat there clicking through the channels on the small flat screen television, wondering what to do with myself, I thought of Maria a lot. I wondered how this would have been different had we grown up together and not been so distant. We were always connected, that is a real thing with twins, because I felt the sharp pang of permanent separation from her right now, but I wondered how much worse that would be if we were best friends like most sisters and twins are. Would I have even met Bobby? I wondered about that, too. Had I had a connection to my home and family in Chicago and not wanted to desperately outrun my past, I probably wouldn't have even ended up in California. I would probably have married a Nick, Tony or a Joey and I'd be exhausted after giving my four kids a bath and reading them a bedtime story right now instead of hanging out alone in a hotel in bumfuck Missouri.

It was mindfucking me. I had to get out of there.

I thought since I hadn't seen a store in years, that some retail therapy would cheer me up a bit. Obviously, there weren't any malls where I was, but they did have the largest Walmart I had ever seen. It had to be as big as seven football fields, and was practically a town on the inside with its row of fast food, the bank, a hair salon, a car repair center, and a little clinic. It fascinated me that you could spend an entire day there doing and purchasing everything in life you needed.

I walked the aisles, and picked up some odds and ends I don't even remember. Mostly I was a zombie with my mind buzzing with thoughts I didn't want to think, and my inner voice screaming at them to go away. After an hour or so, I got bored, paid for my zombie brain purchases and went back to the hotel.

Jennifer Gulbrandsen

I cracked open a beer from a six pack I had bought with my earlier dinner for old time's sake, and used it to wash down some night time cold pills to help me sleep. I had a long day of driving tomorrow and I needed my sleep. I also would do just about anything, including this weak attempt at roofie-ing myself to get the buzzing in my brain to stop for just a few hours. I desperately needed to talk to someone, but the problem was, I couldn't without possibly alerting the National Guard in the process, and I wasn't about to do that to myself.

I felt the buzz of the beer take hold, and the glow of the sleep aid kicking in shortly after. The buzzing stopped and I drifted off to sleep and dreamed of Maria.

CHAPTER 13

I really didn't intend to go AWOL. I really didn't.

I woke up feeling a little bit better, and set out on the next day of driving after a little breakfast of cold cereal, lukewarm milk and a mostly brown banana provided at no charge in the tiny hotel lobby. In order to keep my running dialogue in my head to a minimum, I cranked the tunes in the car and got reacquainted with music. I had a lot of pop music to catch up on, and when I got tired of music, I listened to talk radio so I would know what the hell was going on in the world besides the saga of my crazy life.

As I came upon St. Louis and had to turn north to travel through Illinois, that's when the pang of loss returned deep in my gut. Even though I was a full day's drive away from the place I once called, "home," tears began to roll down my face because chances were, I would never see Maria again, or if I did it would be at least a couple of decades before the coast was clear. I was driving through the last shred of my life as Ava Giancola as I knew it. Ol' Becky didn't have that history. Becky had a clean slate and a nice little house waiting for her out east.

God I hated that name.

I decided to take myself on a quick tour of downtown St. Louis for a couple of hours. I wanted to see a mall, eat some sushi, and just feel normal for an afternoon before getting back in the car and making my way through Illinois.

And you know what? It actually helped a lot. I felt true enjoyment walking through a Nordstrom and sitting down for a dragon roll with a really good glass of chardonnay. I had my nails done and a pedicure, and I felt almost human. I had worn sunglasses thinking a dozen people were going to recognize me, but no one did and it was a false sense of comfort, because as I put my shopping bags in the car and pulled out of the garage I had parked in for the day, I had the false sense of security of a 'normal' life. Maybe I could do the whole 'Becky on the East Coast,' thing after all.

I got back on the highway and crossed over the Mississippi into Illinois, and the sun was low in the sky behind me. I opened a soda I had brought with me to wake me up a little because I had some lost time to gain on the road. I had bought a book on CD and popped that into the stereo to keep me busy. As the opening credits came over the speakers, I looked up at the signs and the first sign I saw said, "I-55N Chicago".

Without even thinking, I took the exit.

* * *

"She didn't check in to her hotel," Garcia said, slamming a file folder on Wilcox's desk as he continued to pack the banker's boxes with his stuff. For an office he barely spent any time in, he sure did accumulate a crap ton of stuff over the years.

"Hmmm," he mumbled as he tried to figure out when he bought this hula girl coffee cup he found in the bottom drawer.

"So you don't care?" Garcia pressed.

"Oh, Porter! Yeah! That sonofabitch! He brought me this thing. What a pisser. Wonder what he's up to these days. I should call him," Wilcox laughed as he placed the mug in the box, "I ever tell you about the luau Porter and I almost got thrown in the tank over? Shit. Those undercover days were insane…"

Garcia rolled her eyes, "Yeah, tell me about the luau you and some other guy almost got arrested at after you tell me what to do about Ava."

"Becky," Wilcox corrected.

Garcia rolled her eyes again, "Listen, I know you are retiring and have one foot out the door, but when you go, she officially becomes my problem, and I would like a little help before that happens. I have two other cases cooking and I really don't want to be occupied by an AWOL Ava."

"Becky."

"Jesus, Wilcox! C'mon!"

Wilcox chuckled, "My guess is she got a little distracted in St. Louis. Everyone we send east who does a little time with us always spends a day in the city. It's therapeutic for them. Gets them used to shopping, dealing with noise, crowds, and the like. You know this."

"Yeah, I do know this," Garcia said crossing her arms, "She used the credit card a couple of times in the city and we have the track on the car up until Marion. Then it goes dead and we haven't gotten a signal since. The phone goes straight to voicemail, and no IPASS cameras have seen the plates since she went into Illinois."

"That doesn't really mean anything. She's in Timbuck Twelve out there if memory serves me correctly. Those GPS trackers break down all the time, and she's probably got a shitty signal in the sticks. I think you're being paranoid. She might be putting the pedal to the floor to get to her new place faster. That's also been known to happen."

"Yeah, but what about — "

"Nah, I would hardly think someone would nab her, especially one of Bobby's goons in the middle of nowhere. Only three people know her file, and two of them are standing here, and no one's getting shit out of Sorenson without waterboarding him. I say let it go, and see if we can get a signal on her tomorrow."

Garcia gave him a reluctant look, but eventually agreed with him and left Wilcox to his packing. When she was gone, he went over to the phone and dialed Ava's new cell phone number.

* * *

"Hey Becky. It's Dan. Call me."

I hit end and threw the phone out the window after listening to the message. After I had made the decision to head towards Chicago, I got a surge of adrenaline like I had made the right decision. I knew they were going to keep tabs on me, so I pulled off to a truck stop and ditched the cards that were given to me, and pulled the GPS out of the trunk, smashed it, and threw it in the dumpster. All of it probably caught on tape, but I didn't care. I would head south out of the truck stop and take some back roads back to the highway heading in the right direction. I had just gotten safely through a whole day in St. Louis, so surely I would be safe six hours away in Chicago. This was overkill and I wanted to see my sister. If only for a couple of days, anyway. Then I would call Wilcox and head to my new life. I just wanted to see Maria one last time.

The excitement over seeing Maria made the rest of the drive go fast. Soon I was on the Stevenson Expressway, and I could smell the Argo Corn Starch plant, while seeing the skyline off in the distance. Planes flew low as I crossed over Cicero Avenue near Midway Airport and my heart began to beat faster. I licked my lips and wanted to scream with glee. I was home. A home I might have hated once upon a time, but a home that was actually mine and not a fairy tale concocted by someone else. It was exhilarating.

I turned off Lake Shore Drive and started weaving my way through the side streets to the pub. When I saw it, I actually did let out a little yelp of glee. I parked the car down a couple of blocks and walked up to the entrance. It was now just past closing time, and when I reached for the door handle, it was locked. I knocked loudly, and saw Maria's head look out the window, and then the door opened. Standing before me was my twin I hadn't seen in years. A little curvier, a couple more tattoos, but she was still Maria.

"Holy fucking Jesus tap dancing Christ on a goddamned cracker. Ava?"

Tears welled up in my eyes and I simply nodded with my lip quivering, running into her with an embrace that was exactly the way you would hug someone you knew to be dead that was still alive. We stood there holding each other crying for a full ten minutes before Maria pulled away, her tear stained face and glassy, red rimmed eyes locked on mine.

"Fuck, Ava. You're so fucked. Why did you do this?"

Because I needed her. I couldn't do this on my own. I really had lied about that.

CHAPTER 14

Maria ushered me in, looked behind me, and slammed the door.

"What in the actual fuck, Ava? What are you doing here?" She yelled while continuing to look over my shoulder out the windows, then furiously closing blinds, double checking locks, and turning off lights. I stood silently watching her hustle around the pub, and then I burst into tears.

"Oh, no. No. NO!" she shouted, grabbing me around the shoulders and ushering me into her office in the back. She sat me down in one of her over stuffed chairs and poured herself a shot of Jack Daniels. Then she poured me one, as I sat there bent over heaving with sobs.

"Ava. Ava, stop. AVA LOOK AT ME!" she shouted again while thrusting the shot glass of smelly alcohol in my face. It was enough to make me quit crying long enough to consider dry heaving. I took the glass from her and downed the shot. I started coughing almost immediately as the liquor burned my throat into my chest. I looked at

Maria looking down at me with a stern look on her face and handed back the glass.

"You need to stop," she said flatly, "This was stupid. I can't believe you're here."

"I'm sorry. I'm sorry. I was driving to my new home, and I was in St. Louis, and the thought of never seeing you again, I just panicked. I wanted to see you so badly. I have lost everything, Maria! My life, my husband," I started crying again, "My best friend over the last few years was an old FBI agent who may or may not be insane, I just had to see you. I couldn't bear losing you on top of everything else. I'm sorry."

She sat on the arm of the chair beside me, and put her arm around my shoulders, pulling me in close and kissing me on top of the head, "I'm sorry, Ava. I know. I am really happy to see you. I am. I have been a wreck over this whole thing, and I didn't know what to do. But now, you've gone off the grid and there is a reason you are going into witness protection. You have really bad dudes looking for you, and now the FBI is going to find you, too. They have tracking on you, you don't even know about. That car is going to be found, and it will lead whoever wants to find you straight here."

"I'm sorry," I said through tears, "I'll get back on the road right now."

"No, no. It's not that simple, Ava. You don't get the luxury of going off the grid and getting back on," she let me go and got up to fix me another drink. "Here," she said handing me another glass of Jack, "You sip on this for a minute, I'm going to go make some phone calls. You don't have anything on you right now, do you?"

"No," I answered.

"Ok, good. Sit tight."

* * *

"She's still gone," Garcia said as Wilcox came into the office carrying more empty boxes.

"And?"

"And now we have to find her," she said tersely, "I told you she was a runner way back when, Dan."

"So you think she ran? If she ran, then why do you have to find her? Let her run and spare yourself the trouble. She doesn't have family or friends, really. She's either going to make it, or she's going to think it's safe to return to San Diego, where I'm pretty sure a Perez goon will kill her within a day. Or, she gets back on the road and gets her ass to where she's supposed to be."

"Honestly, man?" Garcia asked incredulously, "You willing to let her go that easily? I thought she was some kind of special snowflake or something, which is why only three of us are even on this case given what a huge pain in the ass she was."

"That was security, we had a breach," Wilcox replied.

"Whatever. So you're still the lead on this case until 5pm tonight. You saying to let her just run? Years invested in this woman's safety, and you're okay with her flushing the whole thing."

"I didn't say I was okay with it," Wilcox said while setting down the empty boxes, "What I'm saying is, if she is a runner, you let her run and eventually she runs out of places to go. We have her IDs tagged, so she can't get on a plane. We have her money tagged so eventually she will need to eat. I'm simply saying, we wait. You hear from her? Send a local guy out there to give her a stern talking to, remind her that she is in this program for a reason, and get her ass where she's supposed to be. Or you can sit there and wring your hands anyway. You'll be the lead after today, so that's your choice. Right now, I'm packing my last few boxes, shaking some hands, and blowing this popsicle stand for the last time. Ava ain't gonna get too far. If she's dumb enough to get herself killed, then there wasn't anything we could do in the first place."

Garcia shrugged and walked out of the his office, shutting the door behind her.

"Fuck," Wilcox whispered under his breath, "Jesus Christ, Ava. Why."

* * *

"Seriously?" Ava half chuckled, "You thought I was a runner and just left it at that?"

She had been in the hospital for five days now, and she looked a million times healthier than she did right after the shooting. Today she was sitting in a special recliner with a blanket on her lap. The color had returned to her face and her eyes weren't dull anymore. It would be a few more days here before she was put on a rehab floor for about a week to get her strength back, and then she would be able to go home. Wherever that happened to be when this was all over.

Wilcox was standing in his usual spot, leaned up against the wall, "I'm not sure what I thought. I had a gut feeling you were safe, though. I guess I did think you were a runner, or at the very least stupidly impulsive, that was just based on my history with you," he replied then took a sip of his coffee.

"But you understand now, right?"

"Jesus Ava," Wilcox shook his head, "You act as if you're this enigma no one could possibly understand. Let me tell you something, you're not that complicated. Had I known you had a twin sister who was connected, I probably would have looked there first. That's my own shitty detective work to blame. That's why she freaked the hell out when you showed up on her doorstep. She was a smart cookie, that Maria. She probably figured eyes had been on her the whole time, and the bureau was about to get a two-fer on you and her little organized crime operation. But lucky for her, I dropped the ball," he finished his coffee and tossed it in the garbage can across the room, making the shot, "It's a shame I never met her, really. She got you hid better than we did, then was able to bring you back without anyone noticing. That takes some serious skill. I would tell her I was impressed, then offer her a job."

Ava smiled and looked away, obviously pained at the memory of what her now dead twin sister did for her.

"I did have words with Johnston over it, though and made sure my message was heard loud and clear," he said.

"Wait, what?" Ava asked.

"Even though I knew you were okay in my gut, I just wanted to send a message to Johnston that I knew for sure would be relayed to Bobby, that should any harm come to one hair on your head, I would make sure the holy hand of God would come down on all of them, and they'd wish they were never born. I don't usually make those threats, but when I do, they're typically heard. Oh, and I dropped a little bit of a dime on that pussy that got him shipped off to Chicago pushing paperwork for a bunch of cowboy wannabe freelancing fugitive finding Marshals," he let out a laugh, "Which is ironic considering I basically had him sent to your doorstep."

"Yeah, that's really funny," Ava said dryly.

"Not funny, ha-ha, but it's funny like, 'how many ways can I step into a pile of shit and fuck everything up' kind of way."

"I know the feeling," she said.

CHAPTER 15

The way Maria got me out of the country undetected was nothing short of a mission executed with military precision. Within minutes of her making some calls in another room, I was being wheeled out into a van in a garbage can, and in an hour, I was at her vacation house in Lake Geneva, Wisconsin.

"You don't go outside. You don't open a window, and we need to change the way you look. I can't believe the fucking Feds sent you out into the world with fucking highlights. Bunch of fucking morons. So that's first. Pick a look, and we're going to go with it. It has to be something completely different than the way you look now, but not enough to make people notice you. You need to just be different while blending in. Redheads get noticed, so I'm thinking we make you a blonde or something."

"Okay," I answered just trying to take it all in.

"You won't be on the news or anything, because they won't want the world to know that they are a joke, and they also won't want to tip off Bobby's guys to the fact that you're out there in the world unprotected. What they're going to do is wait for you to fuck up and come to them by trying to leave the country, using the money they gave you, the cell phone, the name they gave you, anything like that. If that doesn't get pinged on their radar, then they're going to just assume you're dead or not their problem anymore, and go about their business."

"How long do you think that will take?" I asked.

"Two years or so," Maria responded matter of factly.

I guess the look on my face gave me away because Maria rolled her eyes and let out an exasperated sigh, "Really? You think that you being in Wisconsin somehow made this all go away? Honey, no. They invested time and money into you, and while they won't hurt themselves looking high and low for you, they will keep tabs on you and eventually find you if you stay in one place. Someone is going to recognize you. There are a lot of cat lady Sherlock Holmeses out there who would cream their panties at a maybe-sighting of you in their town and blow that shit up on their little conspiracy theory message boards, completely blowing your cover. Then the FBI shows up, you get charged with something, I get charged with conspiracy, and we get to be cellmates and pen pals with your husband."

I sat there in stunned silence.

"So here's the plan. We get your look changed up, and we get you papers. That's not really hard, because we're going to send you to Nassau and they'll let just about anyone with a piece of paper in, no questions asked. You stay in a nice little beach house, lay low, eat a shit load of conch and drink all the drinks, then we bring you home on a cruise in a couple of years, because if there's a loose border in this country, it's an overworked, commercial cruise line border cop in Miami. After that? I don't know. I don't have a clue."

I was still sitting there quietly, taking it all in. So basically, when this was all said and done, almost an entire decade of my life would be devoted to hiding. Now instead of hiding from a revenge seeking drug lord with the protection of the FBI, I would now be hiding from a revenge seeking drug lord and the FBI with the protection of my sister, who seemed more than up to the challenge.

Maria sat down and put her arm around me and I leaned my head on her shoulder. She smelled like clean perfume with a hint of menthol cigarettes. "This is it, kiddo. You got a raw deal in all of this, but you can make this right, but you have to listen to me. Think of how fast those years with the Feds went and you were in the middle of nowhere. At least you're going to spend your next couple of years in paradise and come back all tan and happy, then wonder why the fuck you came back to a Chicago winter in the first place."

We both laughed for a second while snuggled up on the couch, "Thank you Maria."

"Don't thank me, yet. Thank me when we pull this off."

* * *

Johnston opened the interview door with his keys and the steel door shut behind him. Bobby, now out of a jumpsuit and in regular prison 'blues' sat there well groomed and clean shaven.

"Looks like working in the law library is doing you well," Johnston said forcing a jovial tone.

Bobby sat silent with his eyes fixed on the agent.

Johnston reached into his bag and pulled out a file folder, "I'll just spare the pleasantries and cut to the chase. Looks like we've found a judge, and he's willing to play ball. I already let your lawyer know. Seems like some evidence is going to get tainted, an appeal is going to be granted, and you'll be let out while that happens."

"How much," Bobby said flatly.

"Off the cuff, two mil for the judge's signature, and whatever incidentals along the way. Not really my level of expertise. I paid off the evidence tech, and your test results should be kosher when the appeal gets filed," he slid the file folder across the table, "Everything is right here."

"What about Ava? If I get a new trial she'll have to be called again, right?"

"I'm not sure how that goes once she's been ensconced in protective custody for so many years. They might have her testimony just read from the original transcript at the new trial because they will argue that bringing her into a high profile case like this will compromise her safety. As for where she is right now, I haven't been able to figure that out. Wilcox made my life a living hell at the Bureau on his way out, and now I wrangle a bunch of Mayberry sheriff deputies who want to play dress up in a Marshal's uniform all day and catch a bunch of low level bail jumpers. I'm surprised I even got in here, quite frankly. I guess word hasn't spread that fast."

"Should've been more careful."

"I could say the same of you."

Bobby cast a dark look under his eyebrows at Johnston, "This judge. How long?"

"You want it to look legit, you're looking at two to three years for it to get on his desk. I'm sure more money would expedite the process, but you don't want it to look suspicious. Letting a guy just convicted of a bunch of murders, including the murders of FBI agents, get bail is going to be attention enough."

Johnston zipped up his bag, "So I guess this is it for our business relationship. I thank you for the financial compensation, as it has cost me my career and my wife left me as soon as I said the word, "Chicago," but at least my kids will have a paid college education, and I can live comfortably in the Windy City while working my way back up the ranks. Thank you for this lesson in ethics, Mr. Perez, I wish you well."

As Johnston put his key in the lock Bobby spoke.

"It's not that easy and you know that," he said to Johnston's back, "I call, you answer. Just because your family isn't with you doesn't mean they're always safe, Agent Johnston. I may need you again, but chances are, you'll need me first."

* * *

Wilcox knocked three times on the safe house door and heard the footsteps of the agent watching the house in the tile foyer. The agent was a young guy named Rider, in the Chicago Bureau, who knew of Wilcox's work, and he was impressed at the level of respect the agent showed the old timer back out of retirement to tie up his last case.

"Rider."

"Sir. I have Mr. Mitchell in the dining room waiting to talk to you."

"Okay," Wilcox said as he followed Rider through the front hallway, into an open kitchen with an adjacent dining room. A man in his mid-30's was sitting at the table with his arms folded in front of him in a posture of being complete defeat. He was surprised after dealing with the slight, almost hawkish Bobby Perez, that Ava ended up with this guy who couldn't have been more of an opposite to her last love.

Dr. Justin Mitchell was at least six and a half feet tall and built like a brick wall. Wilcox wondered how he was an ER doctor with those huge hands of his. This guy looked like he should be a middle linebacker for the Bears instead of putting back together car accident victims. This guy was definitely worse for wear as his curly brown hair, worn a bit long on top, was drooping over his left eye, his five o'clock shadow and bags under his eyes revealed he probably didn't do more than sit in this chair over the last five days. He definitely hadn't changed his clothes, as Wilcox could still see Ava's blood on the right arm of the rolled up sleeve.

Justin looked up as Wilcox entered the room and stood to shake his hand. After the initial introductions, Rider left the room and Wilcox took a seat across the table from Justin. There had already been a tape recorder set up and he hit 'record'.

He had Justin state his name for the record and said that this was a purely informational questioning session and that he had no reason to suspect he was under suspicion for any crime and was free to stop at any time. He asked Justin if he wished to proceed and Justin gave his consent. A few more informational questions for the record, and then he relaxed his posture in the chair and began his questions with an informal, conversational tone.

"Well this has been a clusterfuck of epic proportions," Wilcox began.

"For who exactly?" Justin asked.

"Well you, for starters. You fall in love with a woman you think is one thing, she doesn't tell you she was married to a psychopathic drug lord and that she went AWOL on the FBI herself. Her sister gets murdered in what seems to be a random act of violence, she wasn't, you get raided by the Feds, said psychopathic drug lord realizes he's made a huge mistake and now everyone has to die, your ex girlfriend put the wheels in motion for all of this to go down, because she just so happens to want to hurt you and is in cahoots with the crooked agent who allowed the psychopathic drug lord to buy an appeal, and here you are wondering why this happened when you just fell in love with that pretty blonde girl at the hospital, because it turns out she's a liar with a ton of secrets that got her sister killed, herself shot, and you in danger. Seem about right?"

"That's a rather simplified version of things, I guess. But accurate."

"How do you feel about Ava, I mean, Holly, right now? You haven't asked how she is," Wilcox asked.

"I'm still in shock. Angry. Sad. All over the place, really. I keep asking myself if she's really who I think she is, or if she's just a calculating sociopath herself."

"Hmmm," Wilcox began, "What makes you go to 'calculating sociopath' as a viable explanation for all of this? You really think that?"

"Listen, I'm a simple guy of logic. Why in the world would an innocent woman go to such lengths to lie so much? Why would she ditch her witness protection? Why did she lie to you guys about who she was when you went after Bobby? Why go through all of this lying and weaving and creating a whole new person if you're innocent, you know?"

"I can see that. Are you basing those questions to me off something Diana said to you?"

"Some of it."

"Well, I can pretty much tell you anything Diana went to you with was probably embellished and self serving. She tried to get Ava, I mean Holly —"

"Just call her Ava," Justin interrupted.

"She tried to get Ava nabbed by Agent Johnston in Oklahoma before the trial."

"Really?" Justin asked incredulously.

"Yeah, so while in the prism of this shitstorm, she seems like a truth telling saint, she is actually right in the same league as Perez and Johnston. She will probably be charged with something."

Justin was truly taken aback by this news.

"What about Ava?" He asked.

"What about Ava?" Wilcox asked back.

"Will she be charged?"

"Hard to say. She messed everything up pretty badly. I guess we could charge her with something, but what, really? WITSEC is a completely voluntary program, and we didn't have a US Marshall security detail on her when she left Oklahoma, so we essentially provided her window for her. If you were sequestered for years after your entire life blew up, and saw the road home on your way to a new life, would you maybe want to hug your sister one last time and say good-bye?"

"She got her sister killed."

"Her cross to bear, really. I'm sure living with Maria's death and hurting you in the process on her conscience is worse than any sentence a court could hand down. If she had followed the plan to a tee, it wouldn't have necessarily have kept Maria safe. They're identical twins. Hell, I'm here because the M.E. ran her prints and Ava's identity was the only one in the system because we fingerprinted her for WITSEC."

"She still lied. About everything."

"Yeah, she did."

"It came so easily to her." Justin said looking beyond pained.

"Did it though?"

* * *

Two years did go fast in Nassau. I went on a bit of a spiritual journey that involved a lot of booze, and banging a ton of single guys on a day trip from their various cruises. I had never been promiscuous before, but you know what they say, the best way to get over a guy, or a pretend husband, is to get under another one. Or a few dozen. Whatever. I was Holly Gordon, and she was a fun girl in paradise without a care in the world. You would think it a rather empty existence, but after what I had gone through, it was exactly what I needed.

As Maria promised, I came home a couple of years later, right through Miami without any fanfare. My shoulder length bleach blonde hair striking against my suntanned skin, I flew home to Chicago, and took a cab to my new fully furnished condo in Hyde Park. While I was 'away,' Uncle Angelo had died and Maria was now the head boss lady of the family business, and apparently the import/export/money laundering business was doing rather well.

I couldn't dance anymore, obviously, so she asked me what I wanted to do with my more than 50 years left on earth, and I told her I wanted to go back to school. I should have gone to college in the first place, I probably would have met a guy who wasn't a murderer. Who even knows.

So Maria worked her magic, and Holly Gordon was enrolled as an English major at the University of Chicago. I had my cute condo, a Mini Cooper to zoom around the city in if I wanted, a full class schedule…

And a raging case of the good ol' Chicago flu.

Which is how I would meet the love of my life.

CHAPTER 16

It takes a lot for a guy to find you attractive when you're folded over in a gurney making friends with an emesis basin. I had been sick for a few days before I finally hauled my sick ass into the ER.

After an agonizing three hours in the waiting room, my name was finally called and when I stood up to follow the nurse back, I fainted. She let out a yell and when I came to, a giant of a man who smelled like clean sheets, with a horrible tribal tattoo across his bicep, had me in his arms and was laying me on the gurney. I looked up at him and the first thing I noticed after his massive size was his smile. A dazzling white smile with just a hint of a crooked eye tooth on the left side. His eyes were a deep midnight blue, and his features looked like they had been cut out of marble. He wore his brown hair in a gelled messy swoop on top with the sides clipped close, and I immediately deemed him the most attractive man I had ever seen.

Then I immediately realized I hadn't left the couch in three days so I probably had a nice case of puke breath and body odor to make him think I was some hobo they scraped up under the Green Line or something.

"Oh good! You woke up!" he laughed as he gently set me on the gurney as if I were some kind of feather.

"Thanks," I croaked, "Sorry about that."

"The flu gets the best of us," he reached for my chart, "Holly is it?"

"Yes," I answered, wishing he would just leave so I could run some soap and water under my armpits and swish my mouth out with something other than barf.

"Well, Holly, I'm Doctor Mitchell, and we'll get you on some IV fluids right away, and run some tests just to be sure we're dealing with the run of the mill flu and not Bubonic Plague or anything exciting like that. So in the meantime, sit back, relax, and enjoy all the amenities the emergency room has to offer," he walked over and grabbed a corded remote from the side of the gurney, "Like the 5 channels of television you can watch! And if you need anything, hit that exceptionally sexist picture of a nurse, and someone will be able to help you."

He flashed a smile and was gone through the curtains. I was in love.

By the end of my five hour stay in the ER, I felt a ton better, but I was kind of bummed I didn't need another IV bag of fluids, because chatting with Dr. Mitchell made me feel better than I had in years. I could tell he maybe was looking for reasons to keep coming back into my room to chat me up, because I don't remember getting so much attention from a doctor in the ER in my entire life.

Usually a nurse brings you your discharge paperwork, but Dr. Mitchell breezed through the curtain again wearing his winning smile, and carrying a clipboard with my discharge instructions. He was so unbelievably adorable, I totally forgot I looked like a street urchin who had seen better days in the porridge line. After he gave me the spiel, leaning in pretty close, I must say, he took out a business card, and wrote a number on the back.

I immediately felt those butterflies you do when you're a teenager and you just know the cute guy is about to ask you out. I thought I was going to start throwing up again. Instead, Dr. Mitchell flashed that amazing grin of his, and handed me the card. I flipped it over to see a phone number scrawled on the back, and looked back at him, looking rather impish at this point.

"Ok, I'm not a creeper who picks up chicks at work, I swear," he said, "And since you signed the discharge paperwork, I am no longer your physician, and so if you ever want to go grab a cup of coffee sometime, or if you need anything, just let me know okay? I swear. You are the first woman I have ever asked out after she fainted on my shift."

I laughed and said okay, and he bounced out of the room like he just got the best news of his life.

Newly hydrated and medicated, I floated out of the ER with a bit of a glow myself. But mostly because Dr. Justin Mitchell was about to make life exciting again. I immediately dialed Maria's number when I got into the car.

"You had better wait three days!" she yelled into the phone.

No way could I have waited three days. I split the difference and waited a day.

Dr. Justin Mitchell and I were inseparable from that day forward. It would be the happiest two years of my life.

I had almost forgotten what had happened to land me in Chicago with the flu in the first place. Love did heal a lot of that wound.

For the time being, anyway. I should have known by now that a boring life where I'm concerned is but a fantastic illusion.

* * *

It was hard to build a completely different history of my life as Justin and I became more and more serious. I would wince every time I lied to him. It was easy at first because we had both wanted to take it very slow. Me for obvious reasons, and he was just coming off a bad breakup with a local newscaster he wouldn't name.

"Saying her name will conjure her up like a demon," he always said.

I thought that was funny, because it made me tease him every time the news would come on, "Is it her?" I would ask, and he would blush and change the subject. I'll admit, my mistrust was inherent since I had trusted the last man I loved, but Justin was clearly a doctor who worked crazy hours. I even Googled him. Fool me once and all that.

But all of that 'getting to know you' stuff was really hard to take. So many times when it was my turn after hearing about his idyllic childhood in Michigan, and his adoring parents and sisters, I wanted to scream out the truth about my life. I wanted to just spill and say, "My dad went to the joint for low level organized crime, because we're a mafia family. My sister and I were split up, and I lost myself in dance to escape it all. I was really good, so I went into the

The Secret Life of Lies

Joffery pretty much on my 18th birthday, but the attention the press gave me at the time spooked me, so I ran off to the Pacific Ballet in San Diego where no one knew where I came from. I met a great guy there and married him, only turns out? He's a drug lord, and we aren't really married at all because he's a dead baby. My sister, who you think is my cousin and we look identical because of a super strong gene pool, isn't in marketing, she's the leader of my mafia family. Oh and I went AWOL from the US Marshals, my name isn't Holly Gordon, and do you want to be my boyfriend?"

Truth is, he was the kind of guy who would have totally gotten it, too. I just didn't give him a chance. So instead, Holly Gordon took a page out of Bobby Giancola's life and her parents also died tragically in a car accident, and I was raised by my aunt and uncle. Then I went to 'find myself' overseas for a while, and here I am ready to get my shit together in my 30s. It was just a better narrative. No harm, no foul. I would give some innocuous fake anecdote, copy Maria on it so she could back it up, and just change the subject. After the getting to know you phase of things, it didn't matter anymore. We were so in love and I was deliriously happy.

After a year we moved in together, six months after that we were engaged, and I was so excited to be a part of this huge extended family that embraced me and even Maria, and there isn't much to say except that I finally felt like I belonged somewhere rather than joined with a fellow orphan with that being the common bond. Experiencing this kind of relationship with Justin made me see how imperfect my relationship with Bobby was in the first place. I wanted to be kept at arms length because I was always afraid of losing those I loved, which is why Bobby's secrets and lies didn't phase me until I couldn't look away when Wilcox showed up on my doorstep.

It happened under my nose because I was too afraid to open my eyes.

My wedding and marriage to Justin was a complete dream come true. It was a huge church wedding with three hundred people, really only the handful of friends I had made at school and Maria were there for me, but it will forever be a magical moment in my mind. So much so, that I didn't even think twice about our wedding picture appearing in the society page of the newspaper as it was something Justin's mother pined for because she wanted to show us off.

That happy moment would eventually be the downfall of the whole charade.

That newscaster Justin broke up with was a grade-A bunny boiler by the name of Diana Knight.

Remember Diana Knight?

We basically gift wrapped this for her. Right there on the society pages. Not only was that doctor that got away beaming back at her, but she knew the face of his new bride. She looked a little different, blonder, but she knew that the new Mrs. Mitchell wasn't 'Holly Gordon' at all.

And Diana knew just the person to tell. Her old partner in crime and current roommate, Agent Johnston.

CHAPTER 17

In the whirlwind of my wedding and new life, Bobby was granted an appeal based on an accusation of evidence tampering and released on bond awaiting a new trial. My blood ran cold for a minute at the thought of Bobby roaming the streets, probably looking for me, but I squelched those thoughts knowing that if he had the first clue as to where I was, he would've already come and killed me, so there was nothing really to worry about. He would surely be heading right back to prison after the trial, because he shot two agents dead in my old living room.

Also, I had confidence the universe wouldn't put me through this a third time.

Like everything leading up to this point, I was so totally and completely wrong.

* * *

Luke Johnston walked through the door and threw his keys on the small bar in the kitchen. He rubbed his eyes and his temples after another grueling day at work babysitting all of those deputies playing hot-shot bounty hunter all day. Today they dragged a mother of four out of her suburban home while her kids screamed because she had missed a court date on a low level marijuana felony charge; completely bringing high esteem to the federal justice system. The thought of all those meat head suburban cops high-fiving each other over this clearly blood thirsty criminal at large made his stomach turn. You really do reap what you sow, he thought. Get in bed with a criminal, and the wrong agent narcs on you…

Diana breezed into the room with a bounce in her step, and Luke really hoped she wasn't wanting to hook up tonight. They were 'roommates with benefits,' whatever that meant, and the sex was good as long as he didn't mind being called, "Justin" every now and again. Diana was nuts, but she was loyal and it beat being lonely with his kids across the country back in California.

She laid a folded up newspaper in front of him on the counter, and she pointed at the picture.

"Look who got married last weekend?"

Luke looked down to see Justin smiling back at him with his pretty blonde wife on his arm.

"So he's married, and that means you can stop stalking him now?"

"No, look at his wife. Look at her closely," she urged.

Johnston was floored by what he saw. Dr. Mitchell had a new blonde wife, all right. Ava Giancola to be exact.

"Holy fuck," he said.

"Get Perez on the phone," Diana said, "I'll call Justin."

***

Wilcox set a hot cup of coffee on the table in front of Justin. He took the mug in his hands and took a big drink.

"Man you cops make some good coffee," he said.

"I'd take that as a compliment if I were a cop," Wilcox replied. He took his seat across the table and started the recorder again, "So you were on your honeymoon when Diana called."

"Yeah. No cell service in the middle of the ocean, so I didn't get the message until we got to the big island," he said.

"So your ex girlfriend, who is a wee bit nutty in the headspace, calls you on your honeymoon to let you know your wife is really Ava Giancola."

"No, not really," Justin began, "Diana is a bit more nuanced than that. She's a journalist after all, and wants to ask her questions. She's actually very good at it. She just left something vague on my voicemail about needing to tell me something very urgent, and to call her when I got home, because it might be life or death."

"So what did you do?" Wilcox asked.

"Ignored her," Justin answered, "Our relationship was over two years ago, and she was annoying. She always had a reason to call me or bump into me somewhere. I just chalked it up to her usual nonsense and went back to enjoying the best time in my life."

"Did you tell Ava?"

"No, I didn't see a need."

"But she obviously got to you when you got home."

"Yeah," Justin set his coffee mug down, "She ambushed me at the hospital. She had a bunch of files and the whole Ava, Bobby, saga. I sat there in the cafeteria, while she went on and on about how Holly is really this Ava chick, but to me, the old pictures looked more like Maria than Ava, and I just thought Diana was becoming unhinged. Here I've been with…I guess Ava…for years. Met Maria, my family met Maria, hell, my Uncle Walter is a cop and he ran her name because he's a paranoid nut sometimes. Nothing. By all accounts, she was who she said she was. So I told Diana to get bent, I didn't believe anything she was telling me, and then she got this dark look on her face and said something to the effect that the truth would come out, she would be vindicated, and there was nothing she could do now."

Wilcox nodded silently as Justin went on.

"So I get home from my shift, and I tell Hol—Ava, what happened in the cafeteria."

"And?"

"She listened rather stone faced, not acting like any of it phased her, fixed me a plate of dinner, and said she was going to meet Maria for a drink. Next thing I know, the door is getting kicked in, and I'm supposedly getting raided or some shit. My house is getting tossed, and the guy leading the raid tells me that Ava is a wanted fugitive and we're both looking at time if I don't give her up. Then I get hit upside the head and it all goes dark."

* * *

As I sat there listening to what Diana told Justin, it was all I could do to keep my composure and not run out of my house screaming. I should have come clean right then and there, but I knew if Diana was involved, surely Agent

Johnston wasn't too far behind, and that meant Bobby already knew where I was, and I had to get help.

I broke many traffic laws driving to Maria's that night. When I got there, I raced to her door and knocked like my life depended on it, because it did.

Maria opened the door, expecting me to ask her if we were going to Ruby Dee for drinks, but instead I shoved her back in her house, and locked the deadbolt behind her, ushering her into her bedroom and closing that door, too.

"What? What's wrong?" She asked sensing my panic.

"Bobby. He knows I'm here," I gasped.

"Fuck!" Maria yelled, "How?"

I told her about Diana confronting Justin and my history with Diana back in Oklahoma. Maria took it all in and didn't say much while I explained what happened. When I was finished, I stood there gaping at her while she formulated her plan.

"I'll take you up to Lake Geneva and have Justin meet us there. We'll call him from the car. We have to tell him everything."

I still stood there staring at her.

"Yes, Ava," It was the first time I had heard my real name in years, "You have to tell him everything. We'll take it from there. Let's go."

We got in Maria's car and sped up north to Lake Geneva. We called Justin both at the house and his cell, and no one answered. We must have called a thousand times. By now I was completely hysterical, and completely unhinged when we got to the lake house.

Maria parked the car and came around to my side, opened the door and grabbed me by the shoulders, "I need you to calm the fuck down now, Ava. You are safe for the time being. I'll go back to Chicago and make sure Justin is safe. Let's get you into the house, so I can get back and see what's going on."

I nodded and with wobbly legs and a racing heart, I went behind her into the house. Once we got inside, she gave me a small white pill to settle me down with a glass of red wine.

"This is going to settle you down and knock you out for a while," she said.

"You're drugging me?" I asked angrily.

"Yes. I can't have you doing stupid shit because you're afraid and bringing whoever is looking for you right to the doorstep. Take it, sleep, and when you wake up, Justin and I will be here and we'll figure it out, okay? Ava, you have to trust me. I have gotten you this far, and I have never let you down, right?"

I nodded silently.

"Okay, let me see you take the pill."

I swallowed it with a gulp of wine and showed her my empty mouth. She patted me on the head, "Good girl. Now I'll be back in three hours, tops. Chances are Justin just fell asleep and he isn't hearing the phone or something. Don't worry."

She raced out the door, I heard her car start and the garage door close.

I later found out that Johnston grabbed Maria's number from Justin's cell and put a trace on her. We had led him right to our doorstep. It would be the last time I would see my sister alive.

CHAPTER 18

The phone picked up on the third ring.

"Hey, looks like we got her. She's on her way back from just over the state line."

"Is she alone?" Bobby asked.

"I have no idea," Johnston answered, "She isn't with the guy, because he's cold cocked in their living room right now. I grabbed her number from his cell phone, because she called a few times, and then there were more calls from a 'Maria' or something."

"That's Ava's sister, the one I told you about," Bobby said flatly.

"I figured, they were both calling like something was wrong, so I don't know if we've been peeped or not at this point. I'm here outside the house, and all appears to be quiet. Nobody's been spooked enough to call the cops or anything."

"He will be if he wakes up. You should just go in and finish him," Bobby said tersely.

"That wasn't the plan, besides, he thinks we're the cops because we went in with guns drawn and badges out. He thinks his new wife is in big trouble, so my money would be on him trying to find her before calling the cops. As far as he knows, we're the cops."

There was silence on the other end, then muffled Spanish as Bobby spoke to someone else in the background.

"Wait there for Ava, and bring them to wherever she came from over the border, I can be there in a few hours. When you figure out where they are, text Julio and we'll have guys there waiting."

"That's gonna cost you five mil," Johnston informed Bobby.

"Oh really? Now you're telling me what stuff costs? I don't think so."

"No Bobby, I go no further until five mil gets wired to my bank account. This is bullshit. I'm not one of your hired hands who's going to go in and shoot the place up because you say so. I found her, I will give you where that phone came from, and then it's all yours unless you pay me. Someone on that Marshals squad I brought in there is going to get greedy and either drop a dime on me or extort me for more cash to keep quiet. Then I either go to jail or at the very least lose my career. For a second time. You get my family and the career once, not twice."

"Are you serious? Get the fuck outta here with this shit. I'm pretty sure you can handle shit job or no job with the money I gave you, did you forget who I am? I will fuck your shit up backwards, forwards and sideways from here to eternity. This is a game you do not want to play."

"I'm not playing games, Bobby. I don't work for free, so if you want shit to go down smoothly, get on the phone and put the money in the bank. I don't give a fuck anymore. I'm sitting in a car, in the dark, in Chicago, waiting for some innocent guy to wake up so I can deliver him to his death by your hand. Five million or I drive off and my next stop is the Bureau and I sing like a fucking canary. It's your call," Johnston ended the call, and let out all of the air in his chest while his heart raced. He knew he had just signed his own death warrant, but he was completely done with Bobby Perez and his bullshit for good. He had lost so much along the way, his life didn't really matter anymore. His wife left him, he was shacking up with a woman who may or may not be insane, and his kids only saw him twice a year, so it wouldn't be that hard on them when he died.

Oh shit, his kids.

Johnston put his head on the steering wheel and let out a sob. This wasn't some common street thug he was dealing with, this was Bobby Perez. If he were offended, the best way to put Johnston in his place was to go after his kids as a reminder of who was in charge.

"Fuck!" he cried out into the emptiness. He had to do this. There was no turning back.

His car computer beeped and he opened the message. One of the comms guys had tracked the phones and the house both Ava and Maria were calling from was in Lake Geneva, a resort town just over the Wisconsin border. He texted Bobby's guy, Julio, the address, and as he hit send, a set of headlights caught his eye. This street was so quiet, he hadn't seen headlights since they rushed Justin, which was a bit of a blessing in disguise because it meant no questioning or concerned neighbors.

The car was a silver late model Mercedes, and it drove once around the block slowly, disappeared for five minutes, then came around the corner again. Johnston made sure to look into the driver's side window a second time and saw a woman with blonde hair scoping out the place. It was Ava. He was sure of it.

Again, the Mercedes took off around the block and disappeared. When it did, Johnston got out of the car, gun in hand and walked toward where the car had come from in the first place. If Ava knew something was up, she wouldn't be dumb enough to park in front of the house and risk being seen.

Off in the distance he heard a car door slam, and with the grip tightening on his weapon, he quickened his pace toward the sound. As he rounded the corner, he saw the woman walking around the back of the car and onto the sidewalk. It was definitely Ava. Dressed in jeans, flats and a leather jacket with a striped scarf around her neck, she walked with purpose toward the Mitchell home. Her concentration broke when she felt Johnston's eyes on her. It was near two o'clock in the morning, and there was a single street lamp illuminating the corner behind them and the church that took up the block before the row of brownstones was dark. They were the only two souls out there.

The woman's eyes grew large when she saw Johnston, wearing his jeans and tactical jacket crossing over toward her. She noticed the gun in his left hand. Without blinking or missing a beat, she reached in her back waistband and pulled out her own piece, pointing it at him.

"If I scream and a gun goes off, trust and believe this whole neighborhood, including about a dozen curious nuns in that church are going to come out here and wonder what in Baby Jesus' name is going on. Drop your weapon!" the woman called down the sidewalk, "I'm sure as hell a better shot that you could ever hope to be. You will be dead before you ever raise your arm. Drop the fucking gun! Now!"

Johnston did as he was told and the woman moved closer, the light illuminating her blonde hair behind her like a halo, as she moved to the middle of the street where he was standing, gun still drawn, he could definitely be sure that it was Ava. She had aged a little, picked up a few pounds and wore more makeup, but this was definitely her.

"Ava—" he began.

"Ava? Ava? Oh you're going to stand in the middle of this street with a gun and call me Ava? Well ain't that some shit."

"Ava," Johnston began again putting his hands up, "Ava, you are in a shitload of trouble and I am here to help you. You can't leave the program like you did. Not after everything they did for you. You are in a huge amount of trouble. We're talking multiple charges. Just come back to the bureau with me and I will do my best to get things sorted out, " he held out his hand, "Come on, just give me the gun. It's over."

The woman cocked the gun, "Like fuck I'm going with you anywhere. You think I'm stupid, don't you. First of all, witness protection is completely voluntary and people can go back to their lives at any time. Second of all, you're an even dumber fuck to stand there and call me Ava. And lastly, if there was as much trouble as you say, there would be backup listening to this, and I'd already be dead. So why don't you try again."

CHAPTER 19

Maria kept her eyes on Johnston as he stood there with his hands up. This had to be the guy who was on the take from Bobby. She remembered Ava telling her about the beat down, and then the chase through the woods. She wanted to shoot him right there in the street for that alone. But the more of a draw she could be, the better chance she had of getting Justin and Ava to safety.

"Where the fuck is Justin?" she asked.

"He's at home," Johnston answered.

"At home alive or at home dead?"

"Alive."

Maria kept the gun pointed and cocked it, "Describe 'alive' to me."

Before he could answer she saw his eyes go over her head, she turned to see what he was looking at, and in doing so let her guard down. Before she knew it, she felt the air go out of her as the cold concrete smacked her in the face. Before she could get a breath in, she was being dragged to her feet with her arms behind her and once she was on her feet, Johnston's arm went around her neck and began to squeeze.

She fought to flip him over her hip or kick him to release his grip, but the size difference between them became too much. Her lungs were screaming for air and she trained her eyes on the streetlamp on the corner to stay conscious. She had one more shot left before it was over. It would take all her strength to take it.

Maria counted to five in her head and when five came, she used every fiber of strength she could muster to turn slightly in Johnston's grip in order to get a good angle, and elbowed him in the ribs with everything she had. She made contact and could feel her elbow go into the agent's ribs. He was wearing a coat, so it didn't do a lot of damage, but it was enough for him to lessen his hold on her and allow her to land some more hits, setting her free.

Disoriented and gasping, she glanced at the ground for a second to locate her gun, and when she couldn't see anything, she took off running down the street toward Justin and Ava's house.

Her heart was about to explode from exertion when she felt Johnston catch up behind her. He grabbed her by the arm, spun her around and threw her up against a parked car. She felt her ribs crunch as they took the brunt of the impact. Again the air was forced out of her lungs as she slid to the ground, but Johnston had her up on her feet again before she could fall. She clawed and scratched at him with everything she had, but he was still able to spin her around so she was facing the car. He grabbed her scarf and began to pull. Maria's legs went out from under her as the last bit of air was cut off. She tried to concentrate on the white paint of the car in front of her to stay conscious, but eventually that went fuzzy and then dark.

* * *

Johnston released the scarf after he felt the last spasm of life leave the woman's body. He had never killed anyone before and was surprised by how easy it was and how little it affected him. He heard the click-clack of heels behind him and turned to see Diana heading toward the car.

"Is she dead?" she asked.

Johnston leaned over to feel a pulse in her neck, he didn't feel anything, "Yes. She's dead."

"Bobby's going to be pissed."

Johnston felt his gut clench at the realization he killed Bobby's prize. This wasn't going to be good for him.

"Shit," he said shaking his head.

"Well, we've still got Justin in the house, so we'll load the body into the car and tell Bobby that she pulled a gun on you and you did what you had to do."

He looked at Diana perplexed, "Your totally fine with delivering Justin to his certain death? This is your opportunity to swoop in and be his savior. He'd probably marry you after that."

"I'm more interested in saving you, Luke."

There was a pregnant silence between them as they stood in the dimly lit street, the woman's body in a heap at their feet.

"Okay," Johnston broke the silence and pulled his keys out of his pocket, "You go get the car and I'll stay here with Ava. We'll load her in and then go get Justin."

Diana left and returned in a few minutes with Luke's car. They loaded the woman into the trunk and Diana noticed something wrong with the hair on the head of the woman's body.

"Wait a minute," she said looking at the body in the fetal position in the trunk, "Put your flashlight on her head."

Johnston shone the flashlight on the face and head of the woman's body revealing what looked like a blonde wig falling off the hairline showing a stripe of deep brown hair.

"Fuck!" Johnston sighed as he heard the click clack of Diana's heels running down the road to the silver Mercedes the woman had parked around the corner. He heard a car door slam and the rapid click clack of heels running back toward him. In Diana's hands was a purse and a wallet. Breathlessly she dropped the purse at his feet and fumbled with the wallet, pulling out a Driver's License.

"Here," she thrust the card into his hands, "That's not Ava. That's Maria Santini."

"What the shit," Johnston sighed again, "So now what? Fuck!"

"Calm down, we just leave her here, make this look like a robbery, grab Justin and meet up with Bobby. Ava is probably in that house up north and has no idea any of this happened," She reached in and grabbed Maria's arm, "Now let's set her down here, take her wallet and phone, leave her purse, and let her get found in the morning."

***

Justin was startled out of his unconsciousness by a pounding at his door. He had no idea how long he had been out, but it was now dark outside and he had a hell of a headache. It took him a minute to realize what had caused him to be knocked out and a wave of dread washed over him.

As he made his way to the front door in the dark, the pounding continued, "Justin? Justin! Wake up! It's Maria!"

Maria? Justin thought. Why would Maria be knocking on his door in the middle of the night? *Holly*. The pounding was incessant, someone was bound to call the cops if she didn't stop, and after today, he had had about all the cops he could take for a lifetime. The pounding stopped as soon as the deadbolt clicked. Justin barely had the door opened a crack before Maria had pushed her way into his foyer. She was a mess. Her hair was everywhere, she was dressed in Holly's clothes he recognized the striped scarf Holly always wore on these cool late spring nights. But Justin noticed something was wrong with her eyes, he didn't know quite what, but they had little blue crescents in the inside corners, red rimmed and glassy.

"Justin, I'm sorry, but I had to get to you."

"I can tell, what is it?"

Maria threw her purse onto the couch and sat next to it, "The hell happened here? You get robbed?"

Justin, still standing, crossed his arms in front of him, "Your sister happened. Your sister, Ava, to be exact. Not my wife, Holly Mitchell, or your cousin Holly Gordon, but your sister, I'm assuming... *Ava Giancola*."

Maria kept her gaze fixed on Justin as she raised herself from the couch, "Holly needs you."

Justin scoffed, "Needs me? Needs me for what? A sucker? Someone to run her game on? What, she can't find another guy for that? Her real husband, the drug lord, perhaps?"

"Justin, please," Maria pleaded, "I don't think you have any real idea what's going on."

"Oh I don't? I meet a wonderful girl, someone I've been looking for all my life, come to find out, she's not that girl at all. She's just looking for someone to play. Some messed up sociopath that pretended to cooperate with the feds to save her husband, moved across the country for a fresh set of victims, I fall in love with her, fast forward a couple of years, I have the fuckin' US Marshals raiding my house, umpteen people following me, and both you and Holly, or do we just call her 'Ava' now? She just keeps lying over lies, and I'm supposed to help her? I'm sorry Maria, you're good, you're trying to be a good sister, but I'm done. I can't help Holly or this situation. It's just too messed up."

Maria looked around the room, and noticed a locked box on top of a bookshelf.

"Is that a gun?" she asked pointing to the box.

Justin felt that a bizarre question, "Yes. You know I have a gun."

"Good. That's good. Wish I had kept a hold of mine."

She stepped forward and looked Justin square in the eye, "Listen, I know you are very upset. But I don't think you really understand what's going on here. Ava has had her problems, yes, but it's not anything like what you think."

Maria told Justin the very abbreviated version of everything. All about Bobby, why Ava ran, the truth about the FBI and the trial, everything. As she was telling Justin all about what Ava had gone through, that not even Maria knew about until now, Justin sat in a chair, held his head in his hands and wept.

"Why couldn't she had just been honest from the start, Maria? Why all the games and the lies, and all the bullshit? Why couldn't she just say she was in trouble? I would have helped her," he lifted his head and looked at Maria, anger growing in his voice, "I wouldn't have abandoned her, I would have protected her. But now it's probably too late."

"I don't know Justin, I think she believed she was protecting us. She went about it the wrong way, but her heart was in the right place. It's hard to comprehend someone lying to you for the greater good, but now I know. I know it all. And that's why you need to get to Holly...er... *Ava*. Get to her now. Bobby is over the edge, and she is not safe."

"Why?" Justin asked, "What happened? You're obviously shaken a bit, so what the hell happened?"

Maria unwrapped the scarf around her neck exposing the bruises, Justin gasped, at that moment knowing what he was seeing in Maria's eyes.

"There's an FBI agent on the take from Bobby. Agent Luke Johnston. He fucked Holly...*Ava*...up when she was in protected custody a couple of times. Your ex, Diana, was the one who recognized her in the paper. I left her up in the vacation house in Lake Geneva and came here to get you. Luke Johnston killed me in the middle of Oak Harbor Avenue."

The Secret Life of Lies

* * *

Justin startled out of his sleep once again facedown in the backseat of a squad car with his ankles and wrists bound with zip ties behind his back. He could feel the cool hardness of the bench under his cheek. The car was moving, and when he craned his neck, he could see out the window that the sun was rising. He could see two people sitting in the front seat of the car, faces barely illuminated by the lights of the dashboard, so there was no way to know who they were. The only thing he could hear was the low tones of the AM news station playing in the background.

"Police are looking into the discovery of a body in the middle of a residential street in the Foxwood neighborhood. A white female, believed to be in her late twenties or early thirties was found reportedly strangled in the early morning hours. Police are not commenting on details."

Justin startled at the news. Foxwood was his neighborhood. He hadn't been dreaming at all.

CHAPTER 20

Justin set his coffee cup on the table and looked at Wilcox, "You must think I'm a complete mental patient with what I just told you."

Wilcox looked nonplussed, "I've heard stranger things. I once had a psychic get a vision that led me exactly where I needed to be and crack a 10 year old cold case. She saw the cream in her coffee morph into the site where a body was hidden, so the idea of you having a visitation isn't at all beyond the realm of possibility. Seems to me, Maria cleared up a lot of misunderstandings for you, so I'm more curious as to why you're still so angry at Ava."

"Maria lied to me, too and come to find out, she was a criminal as well," Justin interjected.

"Ahhhh, yeah, I guess," Wilcox stood up to stretch his legs, "I guess that depends on whether you're a boy scout and consider illegal to be illegal and put a low level, cook the books, old school family business mobster like Maria in the same category as a sick fucker like Bobby Perez. Truth be told, Maria Santini laundered money and got city contracts for her uncles and cousins. I'm no harbinger of morals, but I wouldn't exactly put Bobby and Maria on the same playing field at all. Crime and morality aren't always mutually exclusive, you know."

"I guess not."

"I mean let's look at you and Diana for a second. You guys dated for a long time, and I would put her way up on the coco-loco scale of criminals, when she has a squeaky clean record. She watched Johnston murder Maria in cold blood, left her to be found on the street, then decided your life was disposable after she exposed your wife's real identity. Maria showed up to save you, and your wife took a handful of bullets for you. You can sit there and act like they're the worst people in the world, but you and I both know the path the hell is always paved with good intentions. Especially when it came to the Santini twins. Diana Knight on the other hand, wasn't just a crack journalist, but she also had quite the criminal mind you could say. The way I've always judged people is by intent. Did Ava and Maria lie and did those lies ultimately lead to Maria's demise? Yes. Did they set out to hurt people and take great pleasure in doing so? No. They just wanted to have normal lives when life itself dealt them pretty shitty hands. It's pretty hard to fault them for that."

* * *

I was in a full fledged panic at this point, since I hadn't heard anything from Maria and Justin in hours and they should have been at the house ages ago. It was early morning now, and I knew in my heart something had gone terribly wrong. I had to get out of there, but I also didn't know where to go.

I went into Maria's kitchen and found an iPad in a stand on the counter. On a whim, I logged into my email account and went through my contacts. For whatever reason, call it paranoia maybe, I had kept Garcia, Sorenson and Wilcox's numbers all these years. I even kept the unfamiliar number Wilcox had called me from when I was off the grid and heading for Chicago. I had written it down before I pitched the phone.

It was a long shot that any of this would work. These days people changed their phone numbers and contact information as often as they changed their underwear. I was also fairly certain Wilcox was probably somewhere in the Gulf of Mexico on a beach where cell phones didn't even exist. But my instincts told me I had to move quickly, so I had to come up with a plan.

I toyed with the idea of calling Garcia first, since chances were she would be the easiest to get a hold of, but I wasn't sure if she would help me after what I had put her through when I was in custody. I didn't know Sorenson enough to make a desperate call to him, so that left a gamble that Wilcox still had the same number, and a phone that would ring.

I picked up the kitchen phone and dialed, my heart racing and my palms sweating. The phone rang what felt like a dozen times until I heard a click, a little static, and a "Yep!" on the other end.

"Uh…Dan?" I said into the mouthpiece.

"Yeah, who's this?" he asked over the terrible connection. It sounded like he was on the road or something.

"Hi, uh…this is Hol— uh…this is Ava Giancola. I'm not sure if you remember me, but—"

The Secret Life of Lies

"Ava? Ava! What. What's wrong?" Wilcox asked urgently into the phone.

"I'm in trouble, Dan. Real trouble. The woman from the bar in Oklahoma, Diana Knight, found me."

"Where are you?"

"I'm in Lake Geneva Wisconsin in a lake house just off the main road. About a mile from the strip."

"Where the fuck is Lake Geneva, Wisconsin?"

"About an hour away from Chicago."

"Jesus. You have a sister? And a husband?"

"Listen, I don't care about me so much, I made this mess, but my sister and my husband are in Chicago right now. My sister drove me here to get me out of there while she figured out what to do, and she was supposed to head back home, grab my husband, and be back here within a couple of hours. It's been ten. I know something terrible has happened."

There was silence on the other end as I heard the road whooshing in the background wherever Wilcox was, "I'm a few hours away," he said, "Is there a car or something you can hop on to get the hell out of there fast?"

"I'm not sure," I answered, "Maybe a Vespa or a bicycle or something. Are you calling me from your cell or a landline?"

"A landline."

"Did you call your sister or your husband from that phone since you left Chicago?"

"Yes."

"Ok," he began, "Get out of the house. Leave the phone there. Chances are, it's already clocked and it'll be like wearing a tracking device. I want you to get into town and go to a busy place. Hide right there in plain sight. I will find you there. Don't do anything stupid. Just sit tight. Can you do that?"

"Yes."

The phone clicked and went dead as Wilcox ended the call. As I hung up the handset on the phone, I heard tires on the gravel driveway. I ran to the back door and peaked out the window. There was a black cruiser rolling up the driveway and inside it looked like a man was driving and a woman was in the passenger's seat. I knew exactly who it was when I saw them, Luke Johnston and Diana Knight, and there was no sign of either Justin or Maria.

My heart sank, but the sudden adrenaline surge I felt in that moment was enough to get me into action. Justin and Maria weren't necessarily dead just because I couldn't see them. They could be tied up in the trunk for all I knew, which made it even more important for me to get out of the house and get to Wilcox.

As Johnston and Diana exited the car, I made my plan to run out the deck door and down the side of the house before they got in. I prepared to go for it, when I saw Johnston open the back door of the car and pull something out. All I could see were feet and ankles…wearing my husband's shoes.

I stifled my initial reaction to scream and ran like a bat out of hell out the deck doors and down the side of the house onto the gravel road that would take me to town. I ran like all of our lives depended on it.

CHAPTER 21

Wilcox ended the call with Ava and immediately dialed Garcia's number at the Bureau. He got her on the line and explained what had just happened on the call with Ava. He had been out east visiting Stephanie and was now in Detroit on a layover that never happened, so he decided to rent a car and head back south on his own. Garcia couldn't believe what the retired agent was telling her.

"So wait a minute, you mean to tell me she went back to *Chicago*? We looked for her like crazy up there and there was no sign of her at all. And there's magically a sister and a husband in the mix now? I don't know Dan, I don't think Ava is anything beyond a half-wit runner, but I have a bad feeling about this. It screams set up to me. This woman lied everywhere but on the stand, and we're supposed to believe her now? How much you want to bet it's a trap laid for us by Perez, who is out on bond now by the way, and she's been in this with him the whole time? She suddenly needs you when you're just a few hours away? You don't think that's just a little too perfect?"

"Nah, not buying it."

"Ok, have it your way. You're going to go save her anyway, so do you need backup?"

"Would be nice," he answered and ended the call. He pushed his accelerator and watch the speedometer click to 90 mph as he tried to get to Ava as quickly as possible.

* * *

I got as far as an old, empty hunting lodge about a half mile up the road when I had to stop and catch my breath for a second. I was in pretty good shape, but half a mile in slip-on shoes at a dead sprint with what I had just seen was enough to make my lungs seize up on me and leave me gasping for breath.

I hated the idea of leaving Justin behind. Seeing his feet being pulled out of that car was almost too much for me to bear. There was no way I could just sit in some diner on the main strip and wait for help to come. I had to do something. If Johnston was now involved, then that meant Bobby would be too and certain death for everyone. Who knew how close Bobby was? He could be in the house already for all I knew, or he had already executed them and was staging a gory scene. I had no idea, really, but there was no way I could play the waiting game with my husband in the back of that maniac's car.

I looked around the hunting lodge, and it looked like it had been packed up after the last season and not used since. It was a modest cabin with only a couple of rooms, and not at all the lap of luxury.

Surely there was at least a gun in there, though. Or a phone. Something.

* * *

As Wilcox made his way through Indiana and saw the signs for the Skyway through Chicago, his phone rang again, it was Garcia.

"Yeah?" he asked.

"Where are you right now?"

"About to cross over the Indiana border into Illinois. I should be up there in about 90 minutes give or take. You got backup called in?"

"Well, Dan..." Garcia began.

"Well, what, Garcia?"

"I just got a call from the M.E. in Chicago. Turns out they got a pick up this morning of a woman Ava's age, strangled in the middle of the street, in some Chicago neighborhood. They ran the prints on the body, and they match Ava's."

Wilcox's blood ran cold, "I just talked to her a couple of hours ago. When was this body found?"

"About 4 a.m. this morning," she answered, "I'm telling you, this is a set up. She's dead, Dan. That wasn't her you were talking to. Something is up."

Wilcox could feel the bile rising in his throat, "You sure those prints matched? Not just a partial hit?"

"99% match," she answered.

"Shit! Okay, I'm still going in because it's no doubt that Bobby Perez had something to do with this, and if we can catch this fucker again, we take that chance."

"You're not an agent, so you aren't really doing anything," Garcia replied.

"Garcia, now is not the time to play it safe. I'm heading in, make sure there is backup!" he yelled into the phone before disconnecting the call. He felt hot tears start to sting his eyes as he thought of Ava dying at the hands of Bobby. All of that work to prevent this from happening and there was nothing anyone could have done to save her.

He pressed the accelerator down even further and hoped no cops wanted to play cowboy today. His phone rang again, a different number than before, but the same area code Ava had called from before.

"Wilcox," he answered.

"It's Ava," a woman's voice said rushed and out of breath.

"Try again, Ava. I know for a fact that Ava Giancola is dead. The medical examiner got an ID on the body this morning, it's Ava, so whoever this is, it isn't Ava."

He heard a gasp and a stifled sob on the other end, "Dan. This really is Ava. You have to believe me. What can I do to prove to you this is really me? Your daughter's name is Stephanie, your favorite color is avocado green, you love classic rock and old reruns of the *Andy Griffith Show*, you stubbed your toe on the concrete frog outside the back door on the patio of the Oklahoma house almost daily. Does that prove it?"

"It proves that you know a lot about me. Unless you can prove how Ava Giancola's fingerprints ended up on a dead woman in the Chicago Medical Examiner's office, I won't believe for a second that this is, in fact, Ava."

Now the person on the other end was openly weeping, "I have an identical twin sister, Maria Santini. She got in trouble a bit as a kid, but I don't think she was ever fingerprinted or anything," now the sobbing had become almost uncontrollable, "What the fuck?! Are you telling me she's dead, Wilcox? You let them kill my sister? Oh my god, that means Justin is probably dead, too. I saw Diana and Johnston in the car when it pulled up and they had someone wearing his shoes in the back seat, and Johnston was pulling him out by the legs. Oh my God, Wilcox! How could you let this happen?" Ava dissolved into heaving sobs on the other end.

"Where are you at right now?" he asked, having to repeat himself louder for her to hear him over her crying.

"I ran for about a half a mile and I broke into a hunting lodge. I don't have time to wait for you anymore," she cried into the phone.

"Ava, listen. Do not leave that lodge. I will be there in about an hour. Garcia is sending guys there right now. Do not leave that cabin, do you understand me?"

All Wilcox heard was the line click and go dead on the other end.

"Ava! Ava!" he shouted into the phone. He redialed Garcia at the Bureau.

"Not Ava. Turns out she has a twin sister named Maria Santini. An identical twin, so the prints would be the same. Run her name through. Also have someone see if there is a birth certificate issued before or after Ava's with the same info."

Wilcox stayed on the line while Garcia had people check into Maria Santini, and he drove like hell to get north as fast as he could. After ten minutes Garcia got back on the line.

"Dan. This is fucked up. How did we miss this?"

"What?"

"Maria and Ava Santini are twins. We found the birth certificates. Maria and Ava Santini's father, Salvatore Santini, went down for racketeering in the eighties. Low level stuff, but turns out, the Santini family is one of the oldest mafia families in Chicago. Again, mostly financial, not so much violence. So your little wounded bird Ava is really from a family who knows their way around organized crime, and she just happens to innocently marry a Costa Rican kingpin? This is a set up, Dan. I will have personnel there, but do not go into this as a rescue mission for her. She jumped us for a reason and ran to Chicago. Now is not the time to listen to poor little Ava tell you how much she's in trouble. She ran to see Bobby when she was in Tahoe. This is not a good girl."

What Garcia said made sense. But Wilcox had different feelings about the matter.

* * *

I stood there crying into the rough log wall of the cabin for a while before figuring out what to do next. Maria was gone and if Justin was still alive, he wouldn't be for long. I was in such a state of shock, I couldn't even wrap my head around what to do next. What have I done?

Thinking that Justin might have a chance to survive made my adrenaline kick back in and push my grief into the back of my mind. I really didn't have an hour to wait for Wilcox to get here, and I didn't know how long it would take the FBI to get backup. I had to do something now. I scanned the room and found the gun rack mounted to the wall with various rifles hanging from it. I had never fired a gun before, much less a rifle, and it would be hard to run back to the house with one in my hand, and it was almost a guarantee that I would be killed before even getting a shot off. I needed something smaller.

I began rifling through the drawers of a small bureau next to the gun rack when I came upon a case that held a gun much like the one Justin kept in the house. I popped the latch and opened the box to see a pistol inside. A 9mm to be exact. While I hadn't fired a gun before, Justin and Maria both had taught me how to operate one should the need ever arise. Justin for personal protection should I be home alone, Maria taught me for this very reason.

Grateful for the unrelated double lesson, I checked the gun to see if it was loaded, it was, made sure the safety was on, and stuffed it in my waistband. I then walked over to the window to make my next plan.

It was a beautiful, warm sunny day and while the leaves and vegetation were growing in, they were still sparse enough to see part of the lake house from my vantage point. Now in addition to Johnston's car in the driveway, there were two black Suburbans behind it. I didn't see any SWAT lurking about, so I had to assume it was Bobby and his guys there to finish the job.

I had to bend over and wretch.

Then I steeled myself and made my plan for what I was going to do next.

CHAPTER 22

Bobby paced the living room floor with a gun in his hand. Justin had been moved to a chair, wrists and ankles still bound, and listened to what was going on around him. He kept his eyes down in order to do his best to fade into the background.

The more Bobby talked and wildly gesticulated as Johnston and Diana explained the mistaken identity of Maria, the less he could believe that his Holly had ever married anyone like him. Before Bobby had gotten there, Diana filled him in on all kinds of information that painted his wife, or not really his wife, as Diana pointed out the problem with the whole bigamy thing, was really just as bad, if not worse than Bobby Perez himself.

"I saw this girl when I was working in Oklahoma," she said, her anger visibly seething, "This is no innocent. You think they just let a girl that grew up in the Mafia take herself into Witness Protection? Hell no, she played them and got caught, so she ran for it. Then she played you for a damn fool. Sure, you won't commit to me for your various stupid reasons, but good ol' Holly Mitchell nee Gordon is a better choice!"

Based on Diana's raging narrative, Ava was a criminal mastermind who was in it for her jollies. She made a very valid point.

Diana quit telling Justin Ava's story when Bobby arrived. At first it was hushed tones as he pointed out the scratches on Johnston's face and the welt growing purple over his eyes, and Johnston had to explain to the crime boss how he had to kill the woman who had her gun trained on him, and he thought for sure it was Ava."

"Fucking moron," Bobby said quietly before launching into a tirade that would last minutes and result in him drawing his gun multiple times and pointing it at everyone's head at one time or another, including Justin's. He only addressed Justin once in his diatribe.

"So you're the one she fell in love with, huh," He sneered with his face close enough for Justin to smell what he had for lunch. Turkey.

"A doctor!" he continued, "Tell me *el doctor*, does she still do that thing in bed where she..." going on to describe something beyond filthy he couldn't imagine Holly ever doing. Even if there were no Holly and only Ava.

Justin stayed silent and kept his eyes fixed on the floor. He wanted to scream in the face of this pig, but he wasn't about to make a bad situation worse.

"That's okay, doc. You and your little wifey, what's she calling herself these days?" he asked.

"Holly," Diana chimed in smugly.

"Holly," Bobby continued, "You and your little Holly will be reunited in the hereafter if there is one. I'm not so sure there is, but if there just happens to be some fairy tale kingdom of heaven, I'm sure you two will be gloriously happy there for all eternity. I know I'll be gloriously happy when I fuck her in the ass and then put a bullet in the back of her head."

"So what's the plan then, Bobby?" Johnston asked sounding increasingly weary. Justin felt like he was just about to give up on the whole thing himself. This was clearly a situation where a guy got in over his head for greed and lost his morality along the way.

"Fucking find Ava, that's first. I got Ramon and Johnny out there looking. No car tracks besides the ones that originally left here last night, so she doesn't have a vehicle. She couldn't have gotten that far on foot, and its a really small town, so I don't think we're going to have a hard time finding her. We kill them, dump the bodies, and get the fuck out of here before anyone notices. It's pretty remote, and the nearest neighbor is far enough away we won't even be seen. We have that going for us. Which is good considering you fucking killed the wrong person," he cast a dark glare at Johnston, "Good thing I didn't pay you five mil for this shit."

"Well, if she comes back, which I doubt, she'll be easy to grab. Those Suburbans and my car are going to spook the shit out of her, so she's probably at the Bureau right now and they'll be kicking in the door any time," Johnston pointed out.

Bobby laughed maniacally, "You really think after all the shit she's pulled with the FBI, they would even piss on her if she were on fire? No way she's going there. She'll come to us. I can feel it."

Justin kept his eyes fixed on the floor and wondered to himself who the woman he loved more than anything truly was.

* * *

Wilcox jammed on his breaks about half an hour from the Wisconsin border on I94. Traffic.

"Fuck!" he yelled at the windshield while beating on his steering wheel. He picked up his phone and called Garcia again.

"Garcia," she answered.

"What's going on? I need you to call Illinois and Wisconsin state police and tell them I'm riding shoulders all the way in and not to stop me."

"I can't do that," Garcia replied.

"Yes you can."

"No Dan, I can't. You aren't an agent anymore."

"Well fucking make me one then!" he yelled.

"No," Garcia said firmly, "We had a flyover the house a few minutes ago and there's activity going on in there. We also saw some guys with guns stationed around the property. I have a crew that's about twenty minutes out about to get in there. There's only one road in, and with Bobby's guys out there, they're going to get fired on so it's a bit sticky. My suggestion to you is to get there when you get there, and be ready to question Miss Ava and figure out what the fuck this is all about. Got it?"

"Yeah," he said as he ended the call. He made a motion out his window to the lane next to him to let him ease in and change lanes, and did this until he got onto the shoulder. When he got on the shoulder, he pressed the gas pedal to the floor and practiced his speech to whatever cowboy cop wanted to stop him along the way.

CHAPTER 23

I hid behind a row of peony bushes on the far side of the house that didn't face the road. Luckily, after spotting Bobby's guys on both ends of the property, I was able to hopscotch my way to the house the way I had left without being seen. When I got behind this row of bushes, smelling sickeningly sweet as they got ready to bloom, I peeked into the window.

I could see about half of the living room, and what I saw was startling. Bobby was there looking like he was screaming at everyone in the room, while brandishing his weapon, seeming to remind them how disposable they were to him and how quickly they could be killed at any moment if he decided their time was up. I then saw what had to be Justin in a chair on the opposite end of Bobby, but I couldn't see his face, just his feet, and they moved occasionally, so I breathed a sigh of relief knowing that he was at least still alive.

I wondered where the hell Wilcox and the cavalry were. They should have been here by now.

I watched Diana, Johnston, Bobby and my husband in the living room and wondered what to do next. I had to startle them, because if I just walked in with a gun drawn confronting everyone, I would probably be dead before the first words left my mouth.

I kept watching through the window when I noticed the front door open and one of Bobby's guys walking in. He pulled Bobby to the side and whispered in his ear which caused Bobby to fly into a rage, walk over to Justin, throw him on the floor and point a gun to the back of his head.

I had to go in now. There was no choice.

I ran around to the back deck door, where I had left before, and threw it open. I took the safety off the gun and made sure I was ready to shoot. I walked in through the kitchen and met Bobby's eyes as he stood over my husband waiting to take his life.

"You had better be ready to die with him," I said as I aimed the gun at Bobby's head.

Bobby sneered at me and I saw both his guy and Johnston point their weapons at me, "You're outnumbered, sweetie. Sorry. But I am enjoying the fuck out of this."

I drew a breath, thinking my heart would explode in that instant, as I squeezed the trigger on the gun and began to walk forward. The sound was deafening as my gun fired and the other guns in the room began shooting back. Glass was breaking, bullets ricocheting off the wood beams, and I managed to get between Bobby and Justin, where he managed to almost empty a clip into my right side. After I went down on top of Justin, I heard just two more shots, then it all went quiet.

The Secret Life of Lies

I looked up to see what I thought was the familiar worn leather jacket of Wilcox standing in the doorway as assorted agents started rushing in behind him. Justin rolled me off his back and I landed on the floor next to him. I was having a harder and harder time breathing and I was starting to slip out of consciousness.

I told Justin I loved him, but I'm not sure the words managed to find their way out. As the light in the room got brighter and the sounds more muffled, I fought hard not to slip away, the last words I heard were my husband's.

"She's been hit! Multiple times, but she's still breathing. Somebody cut my hands free!" he then lay his head on my heart trying to hear for my heartbeat, and then the world went black.

It was a quiet black. Not black like sleep, but black like an enveloping peace.

Justin was alive. I would probably die, but I wasn't afraid. I had saved him.

* * *

"So if you were me, what would you do?" Justin asked Wilcox as the agent topped off his coffee cup.

"Well, you can't pick up life as usual, because life as usual wasn't really true, now was it? I bet Ava could tell you a thing or two about that."

"No, but after hearing all of what you told me, I don't think she's someone I could never love again."

Wilcox sighed, "If I were you, I would take that feeling and see where it takes me. At the end of the day, she tried to make the bad decision right, and she put her life on the line to save yours. Not something most sociopaths would do, right?"

Justin nodded in agreement.

"Shower, go to the hospital, see her. I'll take you myself. Things are going to be sketchy for a couple of days while all of this gets sussed out and we determine what the next step is. Perez is dead, and I can't see anyone else in that operation giving two flying fucks about you and Ava, so it might be the perfect time to start over."

"I'll have to get used to not calling her Holly," Justing said with a nervous laugh.

"I can't believe she picked Holly for a name," Wilcox mused, "She has all kinds of attitude about being called 'Rebecca' for the rest of her life, but she says being called 'Holly' is no big deal?"

"Sir," Justin smiled, "If you knew Maria Santini at all, if she decided your name was going to be Holly, your name was going to be Holly."

"Christ I wish I would have met that girl," Wilcox said smiling and shaking his head at the thought of a female version of him who looked like Ava.

But he had Ava, and he intended to not let her out of his sight again. She was just going to have to get used to that idea.

EPILOGUE

I had Maria buried next to my parents, and the rest of our dearly departed family at Queen of Heaven cemetery right next to her favorite, Uncle Angelo. I came to visit everyone weekly, and what was once almost impossible for me to do at first, quickly became something that started to stitch me up and make me whole again.

The thing about grief, that I had avoided now for thirty years, is that you have no other choice in life but to go through it and come out the other side. You can't go around it and try to outrun anything, because eventually the road ends and the only way to keep going is to go through the thing blocking you. I wanted my sister back more than anything in the world, but I was glad to have had her for those couple of years as we lived like true sisters for the first time since we were seven years old, and while my decisions up to that point were unforgivable, they brought me to her and I wouldn't give that time back for anything.

I also took the time to properly mourn my parents and feel the pain and anger I had avoided for so long. I had always resented my father for making the decisions he had made that led him to the pen, but I now understood how you can make bad choices in hopes of a good outcome. That's all he did, and the apple didn't fall too far from the tree for me. After going through all of this, I now looked at him as a flawed and conflicted man just trying to honor his family and what they required of him. It's a trait that ran deep in Maria as well.

I will always carry around the guilt of what happened to Maria like an ugly baby I can't put down or give away. That's my life sentence in all of this, because I do deserve something be responsible for. I went to a lot of therapy after the dust settled, and although I was reminded ad nauseum that I did not make Luke Johnston strangle Maria on that spring night, my actions did put her in harm's way. I have to own it and deal with it.

So I come here and I make sure all of the headstones have flowers after years of neglect and I talk to my large family like we were never fractured and terrible things never happened to all of us. My responsibility as the one who survived is to live this life and enjoy every second of it. Not come here and continue the sorrow I have in my quiet moments.

I've been sitting here for about an hour talking softly and I hear a giggle off in the distance. I look off into the direction of that giggle, and smile as I see Wilcox holding the hands of two kids eagerly munching on their ice cream cones. The little girl, who just turned five, is a bundle of energy, her shiny brown curls bouncing in cadence to her words and skips. She was named Maria for her aunt, and her aunt blessed her with the same unique energy that would exhaust every adult around her. The little boy, now three, is quieter and more reserved. His sandy blond hair flopping in his eyes like his father's. His name is Joey. Like every other male in my family. I couldn't bear to name a little boy Salvatore, and his father wouldn't let me anyway. Joey was a nice compromise.

Wilcox, or 'Tio Danny!' as he was now known, walked with his charges, still wearing the same weathered leather jacket and a beaming smile on his face. He was the best surrogate father a girl could ever have, and an even better uncle to two little kids who only had family on their father's side. Tio Danny was my family now.

"So, how are the Santinis today?" Wilcox asked brightly when they reached me.

"Oh you know, the usual. Maria's telling everybody what to do and Angelo is grumbling, my mom is cooking ziti, and it's really loud," I said smiling wistfully.

Little Maria walked over to her aunt's headstone. Something that always pushed a lump into my throat.

"Tia Maria! Hi Tia Maria! It's me, Maria! We have the same name!" she yelled at the stone and then proceeded to dance around her aunt's final resting place singing, "I love you, Maria! Maria loves Maria!"

"You guys have a good time?" I asked Wilcox.

He ruffled the hair on Joey's head, "We always have a good time, right my man?"

Joey nodded earnestly while still concentrating on his ice cream.

Wilcox rocked back on his heels and let out a sigh, "It never gets easier, does it?"

"Not really," I answered, "You just learn to cope with it, I guess."

"I know you don't want to hear this from me, but I think they would be really proud of you right now," he said.

"Really? I don't think I'll ever believe that."

"Well, I'm proud of you, Ava. You've always had one thing, and that's guts. And now you're a great mom to two great kids, no matter what bullshit happened along the way, the end came out okay. There will always be regrets of some kind, some you wonder if you'll ever recover from the pain. But then another day happens and what you thought was a shit life and a raw deal becomes something worth living for."

I smiled at him, "So are we talking about me, or are we talking about you now?"

Wilcox shrugged and kept beaming as we both watched Little Maria dance around the headstones for a minute longer.

"Well, we should get going," I said, "Justin will be home soon and I'm sure he'll be hungry after a double on-call shift. Maria! Come on honey, let's go home and make dinner for Daddy."

"Okay Mommy!" she yelled as she kissed her aunt's headstone goodbye, "I love you, Maria!"

I love you too, Maria.

Thank you for this wonderful life.

Jennifer Gulbrandsen is the mother of three children and lives in the suburbs of Chicago. In addition to writing books, she is the co-host of the 'Wine and Sass!' radio show that airs weekly on WLLS radio, and a freelance journalist for many publications. She's also the creator of the website, *Chicago Fit Mom*, and a contributor for the websites: Blogher, SheKnows, and Newscastic.

Jennifer also speaks about her life and writing career to various organizations. For more information about Jennifer and her upcoming projects, visit her website, www.jennibrand.com.

Made in the USA
Charleston, SC
05 November 2015